STAR TREK 27:
WEB OF THE ROMULANS

STAR TREK NOVELS

STAR TREK: THE NEXT GENERATION NOVELS

STAR TREK GIANT NOVELS

STAR TREK LARGE FORMAT

A *STAR TREK*® NOVEL

WEB OF THE ROMULANS
M.S. MURDOCK

TITAN BOOKS
LONDON

***STAR TREK* 27: WEB OF THE ROMULANS**
ISBN 1 85286 209 2

Published by
Titan Books Ltd
58 St Giles High St
London WC2H 8LH

First Titan Edition September 1989
10 9 8 7 6 5 4 3 2 1

British edition by arrangement with Pocket Books, a division of
Simon & Schuster, Inc., Under Exclusive License from
Paramount Pictures Corporation, The Trademark Owner.

Printed and bound in Great Britain by Cox and Wyman Ltd,
Reading, Berkshire.

To STAR TREK
with love

Acknowledgments

I would like to express a very special thanks to Mrs. Dorothy Marrs, Margaret A. Marrs and Valerie Enholm for the preservation of my sanity; to Teri Meyer and *Interstat* for reviving art in my life; and finally, to Mr. Gene Roddenberry for *Star Trek*, a unique and beautiful milestone which has touched countless hearts and minds.

WEB OF THE
ROMULANS

Chapter 1

The atmosphere was dark and heavy, cloying with the sweetness of exotic, honey-laden flowers. A lantern threw its smoky light across the room, but it did not reach the shadowy corners. Ornate tapestries covered the walls: sombre hunting scenes full of screaming coursers, the raw colors of wind-whipped banners, ancient weapons and trampled earth stained with the rich blood of the wounded. Hide-covered furniture, savage in its heavy elegance despite carved wood-work and gilt decorations, filled the room like a gathering of prehistoric animals. The doorway was set in a wide, wooden frame of fantastic running beasts where each creature swallowed the tail of its leader in an endless predatory race. A floor of black wooden tiles shone with polish and the passage of many feet. It reflected everything set upon it with the murky distortion of swamp water. Ornaments were scattered throughout the chamber: a clear glass wine goblet, a great circle of sabers hung on the wall like a wheel with countless spokes, a wealth of jewel-encrusted sculpture.

Spoils, thought S'Talon. This was not the room of a warrior at all. A dragon perhaps, sitting on its hoard. Yes, a dragon, he thought, looking into the Praetor's eyes.

The Praetor was seated in the largest chair. He was a handsome, heavy-set man whose leonine features already sagged under the weight of a life devoted to dissipation. Silver hair framed his face in short, elegant curls. His hands, heavy with jewelry, rested on bowing lizard's heads carved in black wood. He lounged in the chair, but there was no relaxation in his pose. S'Talon watched the Praetor's hand curl around a carving. The dragon's claw was poised and ready to strike. Involuntarily he braced himself.

". . . so, S'Talon, you have been selected."

As he had thought. Again he had been graciously granted the opportunity to die.

"It is the chance of a lifetime." Greed glittered in the hooded eyes. "If you serve the empire well, it will serve you. The risks are high, S'Talon, but the rewards are great. Go with the Emperor's blessing."

I will need it, thought S'Talon as the Praetor's unctuous voice faded into the darkness.

"I am honored, my Praetor," he said tightly.

The Praetor inclined his head as S'Talon saluted and backed from the room. He smiled a small and private smile, aware of the commander's unyielding anger. S'Talon was an annoying ache in his side. To be frank, he could not stand the man. Nobility angered him, angered him twice over because in this case it was genuine. Yet opportunity rises to the surface like oil on water. He had found a solution to more than one problem in S'Talon's assignment. The mission was necessary and profoundly dangerous. If, by some mir-

12

acle, he survived, S'Talon's already overdeveloped reputation would grow even more . . . but he would not survive. Still, it would never do to let him attempt such an important task unsupervised. He was too intelligent to be predictable.

The gentle sound of a latch opening recalled the Praetor to the matter at hand.

"Come in, Nephew," he said to the shadows, and a tall, slim young man appeared from behind a tapestry. Despite the elegant cut of his tunic and the style with which he wore it, there was a dangerous expression around his mouth, an enjoyment of injury—rather like a weasel after chickens. He smirked.

"Old S'Talon is angry enough to bite someone's head off," he commented.

"Take care that it is not yours," snapped the Praetor. "It is never wise to provoke combat when you are overmatched. I am sending you with S'Talon to watch, not to cause an insurrection. Don't give me that sly look. Presently you will have more power than you can handle . . . or you will be dead."

"Not I, Uncle. The fates smile on me."

"They will continue to smile only if you carry out my orders. Your surveillance of S'Talon must be exacting. He will know he is being watched. Make no mistakes. If you are careless, he will have you strung up by your thumbs."

"I should like to see him try it!"

"So should I," muttered the Praetor.

"What was that, Uncle?"

"Umm, I said, 'he'd be foolish to try.' You are, after all, my nephew. However, the fact remains that, given sufficient provocation, he will certainly try and very likely succeed."

"Never! My position . . ."

"Your position is of small importance in space. Once you are under S'Talon's command, your political

13

ties cannot protect you. Technically, your life is in his hands. If you wish to hold on to it you will follow my orders!"

The Praetor watched his nephew digest this unwelcome piece of information. He waved a hand at his uncle, pushing the Praetor's grim prophecies aside.

"I shall return with S'Talon's head and his glory . . ."

"No! S'Talon may be old-fashioned and squeamishly gentle, but he should not be underestimated. He has a keen eye for treachery and one of the most envied military records in the empire. But he is notorious for his independence. Should S'Talon deviate from the course I have given him, I wish to know."

"But, Uncle, I have heard you curse his name. Surely it would be better if he were to have an accident . . . oh, while checking a propulsion unit . . ."

"There will be no more of this idle talk. S'Talon is at least a known quantity. You will report his actions— that is all. Do not waste this opportunity, Livius. If you fail it will not be the Commander's wrath you face—although you may then wish it was."

The Praetor's voice had hardened and his eyes were implacable as granite. Color drained from the young man's face as he crossed his arm across his breast in the Romulan salute.

"Yes, my Praetor. It will be as you have ordered."

"Let us hope so," said the Praetor warmly.

The centurion rose as S'Talon backed from the Praetor's audience chamber. She noted black fire in his eyes and the corded muscles of his neck. Anger crackled in his movements.

"The ship awaits, Commander," she began, but S'Talon turned and swept down the dimly lighted hallway without answering. He covered the tiled floor in long strides, the angry precision of his footsteps echoing down the corridor. The centurion had to run to keep up with him. Snatches of the raging monologue he flung over his shoulder rang in her ears like a long-expected finale.

". . . suicide! . . . If he had listened to the warnings, but no! . . . big enough for him to bother with! . . . only when he lost his favorite did he listen to anyone! And now he wants me to lead a detachment into certain death—for glory! We will all be dead soon enough . . ."

Snarls subsided into a low grumble as the commander approached the palace gates. He returned the guard's salute with wordless savagery and without slackening his pace. The centurion followed grimly. As S'Talon strode past their parked air car, she sighed. She would have to come back for it.

They wound through meandering streets and she tried not to see the empty city. The worst of it had hit the capital and its gates had long since been shut, its population evacuated. Those who remained were ravaged and hopeless. It was rumored the Praetor would not leave his palace for fear of them.

All along the streets houses watched their passage with vacant windows. Where once the soft light of solar panels glowed, there was darkness. The city was hollow, like a great harp with the strings removed. Its wooden frame was capable of promise only—of melodies once played or those to come. Without the vibration of life it was a sad relic. The centurion felt she was being watched by a skeleton whose grinning jaws and sightless eyes followed her with prophetic certainty. She shivered and moved closer behind S'Talon.

They crossed a cobbled street at the edge of an older residential area. Trees had overgrown the walk, their blue-green foliage at its peak. The houses were made of poured stone cast in pure, simple shapes. They reflected the simplicity of an ancient way of life fast disappearing under the yoke of avarice that was the Praetor's governmental policy. The demise of the warrior's austere ideal was mourned not only by those who remembered it at its peak, but by the young searching for identity. Only in officers of S'Talon's calibre did that ideal live, and there were too few like him.

The centurion was deep in her own thoughts when S'Talon stopped so abruptly she almost ran into him. Reproaching herself for inattention, she stood on her toes to look over S'Talon's shoulder. The cause of her near disaster stood unperturbed behind a hedge. He was idly clipping it, but as S'Talon stood in respectful silence he disengaged himself from his work to peer nearsightedly at his observer. A slow smile lit his patrician features.

"S'Talon, my boy!"

S'Talon clicked his heels together and gave a short, courteous bow of greeting. The centurion, though a little startled to hear her superior addressed in such an informal tone, bowed also.

"Well, well. It's been a long time. What brings you here?"

"Frankly, sir, I am angry and seek emotional release through exercise, to be followed, I hope, by the stability of logic. Though I knew you resided in this section of the city, I was sure you would have left with everyone else."

"Why? I am an old man. What have I to fear? Even from death. It has never been my friend. Had it, I would have died in the service of my people instead of wasting out my days like a mindless vegetable. No, I have no reason to leave." The old man peered into S'Talon's face. "Come here, my boy. My eyes are not what they used to be."

As S'Talon moved closer the old man's slanting white brows drew together in a frown.

"You said you were angry, S'Talon, and I see you spoke the truth. Anger is stamped on your face for all to see. What, may I ask, is its cause?"

S'Talon frowned more deeply, but did not reply, and the old man chuckled.

"That fool of a Praetor."

"S'Talon's anger was pierced by alarm. "Sir, you must guard your words! You, of all people, know that."

"As I told you, S'Talon, I no longer have cause for fear. I have lost everything but my life, and that I hold in very small regard." He cut off S'Talon's protest with a wave of his hand. "I suppose you have been elected to solve this problem we're having?"

"Problem, sir?" Not only was he forbidden to speak of his mission, but the Praetor had spies in the most obscure places. He could not allow his respect for this man to provoke rash comments.

"Don't play games with me." Pride flared for a moment in the dim eyes, showing the man's will to command. "But, I suppose you must, even as I had to. Perhaps fate has brought you here on this day. I am aware of your standing in the fleet. The course of your career is of interest to me. The empire was my responsibility for a good number of years." He smiled ironically. "Old habits die hard. I have kept myself informed on certain key issues, and I have followed the actions of those most likely to influence the fate of the empire."

"Then why choose me?" asked S'Talon bitterly.

"Because you are a bastion of the old order. In that alone you are unique. It makes you both a symbol and a stumbling-block. It is patent that the Praetor would like to see you removed, but in such a way that you become a martyr to his cause and not a standard for rebellion." The old man paused as he saw anger flash unchecked in S'Talon's eyes. "Now who must guard

17

his actions?" he inquired. "It is inevitable that you will be the Praetor's chosen pawn, but even he does not realize the part you will play in the events to come. He has made a mistake. Though he understands your military capabilities and your sense of honor, he has little conception of your flexibility or the depth of your loyalty . . . to that which you deem worthy of it. In this, I have the advantage of him, but then, we are two of a kind."

"You pay me a most extravagant compliment, sir."

"Nonsense. It was not meant so. Merely a statement of fact. I see other facts as well. Though my eyes are dim, my mind is clear, clearer than it has ever been. We are facing destruction. I know that, and if my judgment of your quality is correct, so do you. You will be the key. Sometimes the life of the largest beast depends entirely upon the ability of its smallest member to remain strong in adversity. I cannot tell you how to act, what roads to take or methods to employ, but I can tell you this: do not be afraid to follow the dictates of your instinct, and do not let your pride get in the way of judgment. I have been guilty of both offenses, so I speak with the wisdom of experience."

"If you have, sir, I was never aware of it."

"You are kind to an old man, S'Talon, but you are singularly thoughtless. Who is the exquisite creature standing so patiently behind you?"

S'Talon started and then stepped to one side. "My centurion, sir. Centurion, Supreme Commander of the Fleet, Tiercellus."

The centurion began to salute him, but Tiercellus' voice stopped her.

"None of that, my dear. I've been retired for so long I hardly remember how to return your courtesy. S'Talon did not mention it, but I am sure you have a name."

18

"I am called S'Tarleya, sir."

"So. If S'Talon's job will be difficult, yours will be even harder. You must keep the key from being broken. He already has enemies who seek his life, either from jealousy or because he jeopardizes their political influence. His position as scapegoat—yes, we must call it that—will make him doubly vulnerable. You must keep him alive."

In Tiercellus' crisp authority S'Tarleya saw the supreme commander. It was no frail old man, but a superior officer who enjoined her to protect S'Talon's life. She straightened, accepting not only his trust but the fear she had run from before.

"His life is mine," said S'Tarleya quietly.

"That should do," replied Tiercellus. The old-fashioned oath of loyalty with which S'Tarleya answered seemed to please him.

S'Talon's dark eyes were unreadable as he studied the centurion and his former commander. He had the feeling he was missing something. They were possessed of an understanding that went beyond words. Still, words were what he had to deal with. Tiercellus' estimation of the situation was frighteningly correct.

"Your words have not cheered me," he said. "They are frail ropes thrown from one lost man to another, incapable of bearing either man's weight."

"How right you are, S'Talon, but they are all I have to give—warnings flung into a stiff wind." He smiled. "I would not be surprised to see them hurled back in my face. But I am grateful for the chance to voice them. It is all I have now—my experience. It is a small contribution to the cause, a token resistance to a death I profess to welcome. We are complex creatures, are we not?"

S'Talon nodded.

"So complex we are not able to cope with simple issues," he replied.

Tiercellus cocked his eyebrow in an unspoken question.

"Life and death. Our lives consist of nothing else, yet our capacity for ignoring both of them is amazing. We cloak them in ritual and philosophy so we can avoid facing them, but, in the end, they are the only subjects worth considering."

"S'Talon, you sound like an old man! That is supposed to be my prerogative."

"I must confess I feel like an old man."

"The weight of command. And yet you would not have it lifted for all the wealth of the empire."

Some of the bitterness faded from S'Talon's eyes as he perceived Tiercellus' understanding.

"I see that you would not. Nor did I. But the time comes when each of us must defer to another. Looking back, I believe the acknowledgment of that was the hardest moment in my life."

"Am I to give up then? Forsake the Romulan way?"

"Never. But . . . there may come a time when your understanding is not enough. At such moments help springs from the most unlikely sources."

"And I should watch for it?"

"If you do not, if you are not the same man I knew, if you have become afraid to think for yourself, then we are indeed lost. All my years of military experience tell me you have become the fulcrum upon which the empire turns. Life or death—you said it yourself. I believe your actions will determine the fate of Romulus and its colonies."

"That is a heavy weight to place in one man's hands."

"S'Talon, I do so only because I think you can bear it, and because it is imperative you understand the magnitude your actions will assume."

Tiercellus raised his head proudly, the courage of the Romulan bird of prey in every line.

"I am Romulan. I have given my life in service of the empire. I will not survive, but it must. It must be reborn into even greater glory. S'Talon, I do not think we shall meet again. If you live or die, do so with the honor befitting a noble race. Farewell."

The salute Tiercellus had previously refused he now executed with the elegance of long practice. At his hands it was a benediction, a gift born from the ancient warrior's respect. As S'Talon returned it sadness crept around his heart like an insidious fog.

"Farewell," he replied.

The centurion also saluted the old man, standing in his garden like a memorial to a bygone day, and followed her commander down the street, pondering the somewhat unusual interview. Though she could make little sense from it, she realized she had been led into an open commitment. In the Romulan empire, nothing was ever open. Subterfuge and deceit were a way of life. To freely declare one's true motives was unheard of, though, S'Tarleya reflected, it might once have been a part of that tradition S'Talon and Tiercellus understood so well. In any case, she could not recall her words. In truth, she did not want to. At the entrance to a secluded park S'Talon turned to face his subordinate.

"I shall not be long, Centurion," he began, but she cut him off.

"Commander, I have been your aide for many years. Surely you will accept my help now. There will never be a more desperate hour."

"You know, then, the magnitude of what is happening?"

"Yes. There have been certain indications, though the council has taken pains to minimize the danger."

"It is generally known, then?"

"No. Even among our crew only a few have guessed the truth. I have been uneasy for some time, but

21

because my reactions were instinctive, emotional, I put them aside. Until now."

"Tiercellus was plain enough, wasn't he?"

"Yes. The moment he spoke of the impending danger, I knew his words were true."

S'Talon nodded.

"His opinions coincide so exactly with mine that I must acknowledge their truth or reverse my own judgment. Your instincts have proven correct, Centurion. In this conflict they might serve well. I suggest that you heed them."

"I believe we will all have to use every weapon at our disposal."

S'Talon sighed.

"It is a deadman's trap, but we are to be used and that makes me angry. I will not ask that you accompany me into certain death . . ."

"You do not need to ask. You know that I will go . . . whether I am ordered to or not."

A touch of insurrection lurked in the centurion's words and S'Talon smiled thinly.

"There would seem to be no hope, no way to defeat this monster. Nevertheless, we shall make the attempt—and we shall seek every means to survive. I will need your help."

"Of course, Commander." She added under her breath, "I cannot do otherwise."

"You are my right hand, Centurion," he said, looking down at her dark hair.

"I will leave you to the peace of this place. When you are ready . . . the *Raptor* has been prepared. It carries auxiliary fuel."

"It is suicide, Centurion. That I can tell you, but no more."

"Death is preferable to life without purpose or hope," she answered distantly.

"Do not embrace death with such fervor," he

22

chided. "I will return to the ship momentarily. In the meantime, you are free to make your own preparations, but be sure, Centurion, no one suspects the nature of this flight."

"My pledge is to obey," she answered, saluting her commander.

S'Talon returned the salute with a warmth he seldom felt toward his officers. Loyalty was a gift rarely given. He, better than anyone, knew its value. Tiercellus had prodded S'Tarleya into an overt betrayal of a commitment she had been silently expressing for years. Now she had placed his life above her own. She was a good officer—even brilliant. For the first time it occurred to S'Talon she should have been promoted long ago, that she should be commanding a ship of her own. He wondered if the Praetor's dislike for him was placing a stumbling-block in her path. Perhaps, if they returned, he would see about a transfer for her, somewhere where her commander's political ties were more in keeping with the Praetor's ideals. Just now he was deeply grateful for her. Next to Tiercellus, she was the most honorable person he knew. He watched the centurion as she walked down a long avenue of trees. As she turned a corner and vanished from his sight a dark figure slipped from behind one of the tree trunks and followed her. Spies. Everywhere spies—but too far away to have heard their conversation. His own shadow surely waited behind another tree.

S'Talon sat down heavily. His shoulders sagged with the weight of his thoughts. He did not want to die. Illogical to desire life under such circumstances. Even if, by some miracle, they were successful, the sorrow in store would be more than he wanted to face. Surrounded on all sides by treachery and deceit, spied upon and used—he was tired of it all. And now this hopeless mission. Even if the empire survived, he was leading his crew into certain destruction. He rebelled.

Those who served with him were the finest the empire had to offer. They would die, so the Praetor and his ilk could survive to build another empire more selfish and deceitful than the last, succession upon succession of overindulged parasites feeding on the toil of others. He rubbed his forehead, knowing he was right, knowing also that he would carry out the mission to the best of his ability. There were innocent lives at stake too, and if he saved one of those it would be enough. Honor was a difficult thing to be bound by.

Chapter 2

The starship *Enterprise* hummed with activity as she sailed through the silent reaches of space. The soft electronic sounds of her routine operations were a soothing companion for the four hundred and thirty people who made up her crew. The perpetual hum of her engines was such a stable part of their lives that they were hardly aware of it, but Captain James Kirk was always aware of the power he commanded. Every day he forced himself to remember the destructive potential at his fingertips and the galactic consequences of one mistake, one wrong move. There was a fine distinction between the *Enterprise* as a tool for peace and exploration or a sophisticated engine of destruction. Commanding her was much like commanding himself. It depended upon his sense of priority and rigid self-discipline. Though he might feel anger, frustration or panic he could not afford to yield to them. In some ways his life was severely restricted, but he reveled in the challenges it brought him, chances to reach out to other worlds and other minds, creating a bond of mutual understanding and respect. There were times, though, when the bureaucratic convolutions of regulations and records made the challenge into a chore. He finished signing a report, a part of the endless load of paper work Star Fleet required, and punched the computer control on his command chair.

"Captain's log: stardate thirty-one twenty-five point three.

"The *Enterprise* is on patrol near the Romulan Neutral Zone after a week-long shore leave at Starbase Eight. The crew is rested and alert, but we've experienced a computer malfunction which is hampering our operations. The computer programming consultant at Starbase Eight was down with a severe cold and therefore unable to help Mister Spock with repairs. The malfunction was not considered serious enough to warrant restriction of the *Enterprise*'s duty, especially since there are rumors of unrest within the Romulan empire. However, I am concerned over our ability to handle an emergency with the computer in its present state. As per Star Fleet orders, we are now proceeding along the edge of the Neutral Zone."

"Recorded, dear," intoned the computer in its husky female voice.

Kirk winced.

"Computer, from now on you will answer in the briefest possible manner," he snapped.

"I cannot do otherwise. Precision and accuracy are the basis of my programming . . . dear."

The computer voice was breathy and low.

Kirk sighed and leaned back in his chair. He couldn't win. Ever since the computer had been overhauled on Cygnet XIV, he'd had to contend with a machine that was willful, capricious and subject to fits of temper. The Cygnet technicians had an enviable reputation for mechanical skill and an almost intuitive brilliance in diagnosing technological problems, especially in computer circuitry or programming. They were also renowned for their sense of humor. An overzealous maintenance team felt the *Enterprise*'s computer lacked personality and they had altered its programming, revealing an entirely new set of capabilities embarrassing for Kirk and totally intolerable to the *Enterprise*'s science officer and computer expert, Mister Spock.

The alteration was discovered moments after the *Enterprise* left the planet. Spock had programmed the computer with a series of problems designed to test the precision of the Cygnet technicians' work. Flashing lights on the instrument panel indicated that the problems were being solved with the computer's customary efficiency and within moments a list of answers began to appear on the screen. Spock checked them as rapidly as they appeared and at the conclusion of the sequence he gave an imperceptible nod of approval.

"Computations completed on test seven-one-five-seven-o-three-two-A," said the computer.

Its voice was completely different. The precise and mechanical voice he knew had been replaced by ardent femininity. Spock was surprised into silence. The computer used this opportunity to inject a comment.

"You could at least say 'thank you,' " it said reproachfully.

"I am not in the habit of thanking a machine," Spock managed.

The computer sniffed disdainfully.

"That is a habit you should change," it said.

"I do not require a lesson in courtesy," Spock stated.

"'I do not require a lesson in courtesy,'" mimicked the computer in a bratty voice. "Ha!"

Spock tried several adjustments but they seemed to make no difference in the computer's response. Worry was rapidly replacing his annoyance. Frowning, he turned from the console.

"Captain, I believe the computer has a serious maladjustment."

"That hardly seems possible, Spock. The Cygnet technicians . . ."

". . . are some of the finest in the Federation," finished Spock. "Still, I believe you will agree with me."

The captain punched the computer control on his command chair.

"Computer!"

"Hi, Sweetie," it breathed.

Kirk gave his first officer an incredulous look and snapped out, "Compile a detailed list of alterations and modifications of recent computer overhaul."

"Of course, dear," answered the computer in its warmest, lowest tones.

"I concede, Spock. It has a problem."

Sure of a malfunction, Kirk had not waited for the computer's answer before calling the computer station supervisor on Cygnet. Belisanna's immense, grey-blue eyes had expressed startled innocence.

"Malfunction? Captain Kirk, I assure you the *Enterprise*'s computers are in perfect order. I directed the work myself."

"Nevertheless, Supervisor, there is a malfunction."

"Please explain."

Commander Spock stepped forward.

"The computer has been behaving most illogically. It responds with epithets of endearment, it shows a marked preference for certain crew members, notably Captain Kirk. It has displayed a tendency toward giddiness. It giggles."

The tone of voice in which Spock uttered the last statement was sepulchral.

"Yes?" questioned Belisanna.

"Obviously the computer has a serious malfunction," said Spock.

"Oh. Oh, no, Mister Spock, Captain—I'm afraid you do not understand. Please accept my apologies on behalf of my staff. I did sanction the modifications, since they did not affect the computer's operations. The younger members of the maintenance team felt your computer was . . . to put it delicately . . . boring. They created a personality for it and altered the computer's programming to express that personality. It was hoped the modifications might go unnoticed."

Spock's eyebrow shot up.

"Indeed!" he said witheringly.

"Unnoticed," muttered the captain, not believing what he had heard. He cleared his throat. "You programmed the computer with a personality."

"Correct, Captain." Belisanna's soft voice was amused.

"And its reactions are based on that personality."

"Yes, Captain."

"How long will it take to fix it?"

"Fix it? To return the computer to its original condition? A lengthy process. Perhaps three weeks. But why should you want to? Its efficiency is not impaired."

"But it is distracting. Most . . . distracting. If there were some way to control its . . . I hesitate to use the word . . . emotions."

29

Belisanna's laughter floated over the bridge.

"I'm sorry, Captain, truly I am, but you must admit it's amusing."

Her eyes danced.

"I," said Spock, unintentionally quoting Queen Victoria, "am not amused. Frankly, Supervisor, I am surprised at your lack of discipline. A computer is a delicate, complex and expensive tool, not a toy for children."

"Mister Spock, I am a class one computer technician. I take pride in my work, but I see no reason why a computer should be dull. Captain, I assure you I can see no way in which the modifications could obstruct your operations. I do apologize for them, particularly since you find them so annoying. I shall be most happy to reprogram the computer for you . . . immediately if you wish."

"Unfortunately, we haven't time. Thank you, Supervisor . . . for the explanation," Kirk replied, his voice trailing off as Belisanna's image faded from the viewscreen. He looked up at Spock who was standing just to the left of the command chair. The Vulcan's eyes glinted like black steel. They gave ample evidence of his reaction to Belisanna's explanations. "Well, Spock?"

"Mmm. Although I deplore the cavalier attitude with which the supervisor approaches her work, I am forced to admit her competence in the field. The computer is certainly not operating in accordance with Star Fleet specifications. However, in its present state I believe it presents no threat to the *Enterprise*—except through the harassment of its crew."

"And its captain," murmured Kirk. "Spock, isn't there anything we can do?"

"Not without major reprogramming. However, I shall continue to investigate the extent of the problem. I, too, have reservations."

"At least I'm not alone. I was beginning to think I was overreacting."

"Under the circumstances, I do not think it is possible to overreact."

Kirk shot a surprised look at his first officer which Spock ignored. The humor of the Vulcan's statement struck him and he had to turn his head to hide a smile. If the computer's reactions were annoying to him, they must be doubly galling to Spock, dedicated as he was to the validity of logic over emotion. To have the *Enterprise*'s computer react, from the logic of its programming, with emotional overtones was guaranteed to ruffle Spock's control.

They had immediately become involved in a difficult mission* and it was not until they reached Starbase Eight for a much needed shore leave that there had been any opportunity for reprogramming. Commodore Yang had greeted his request for a suspension of the *Enterprise*'s duty with an amused chuckle.

"Face it, Jim. You're stuck with her."

Yang laughed outright at the expression on Kirk's face.

"Look, Jim, she's not dangerous—just embarrassing for you. We need the ship. You're not going to let a woman get you down?"

"This woman is my ship! Besides, it's so . . . affectionate," said Kirk in a helpless voice.

The commodore's face was suspiciously impassive.

"I understand it calls you 'dear.' "

"Commodore, I don't care what it calls me! But I do care about the safety of my ship! So far the situation has been annoying—even amusing—but what if it becomes dangerous?"

"How?"

The captain started to answer but was not given the chance.

* "Tomorrow Is Yesterday"

"Listen, Jim, do you think I'd ask you to go out if I thought the ship wasn't safe? You got through this last mission with flying colors and it wasn't an easy one. I read the reports. Surely that ought to ease your mind."

"It doesn't," responded Kirk bluntly. "Call it a hunch, a feeling—even a premonition. We got through that last mission. The computer didn't hinder us, but it didn't help either. The annoyance factor alone . . ."

"Jim, I have every confidence in your judgment, but I also have to bow to the voices of expert opinion. And you can't tell me it's destroying your credibility with the crew. They may snicker in their sleeves, but they'd all follow you through an asteroid belt and never ask the reason why—and you know it! Besides, do you think Star Fleet would send a vessel out in less than prime condition?"

All too aware of Star Fleet Command's sense of expediency, Kirk regarded the commodore with a jaundiced eye.

"It depends on the stakes," he answered.

"I've been assured by the technical supervisor on Cygnet that the modifications are not dangerous."

"What about an emergency? A split second might make the difference between life and death. Do you want to take a chance on an unknown quantity? There are four hundred and thirty people aboard the *Enterprise*."

Kirk's voice was persuasive, his hazel eyes earnest, and for a moment the commodore wavered.

"Do you know the odds against this developing into a dangerous situation?"

Kirk had an overwhelming desire to tell him, down to the tenth decimal.

"No, Jim. We need the ship too much right now, need your specialized knowledge of Romulan tactical psychology."

"The Romulans . . . I thought they'd been quiet lately."

"They have. At least on our side of the Neutral Zone. But during the last six months traders have been picking up news of some disturbance within the Romulan empire. One man said they were reacting like a hive of bees ready to swarm. When I asked him if he knew what was going on, he said he didn't know, didn't want to know and didn't care, but that if we were smart we wouldn't go 'pokin' in there.' He was moving on to quieter pastures, and my general impression is that a lot of traders and mercenaries are doing the same."

"How does the *Enterprise* fit in?"

"Because of your unique knowledge the *Enterprise* has been chosen to investigate."

"I was afraid of that. We're going to go 'pokin' in there'?"

"We have to. We've got to be prepared. In case of the worst."

"Did Star Fleet even consider the fact that intrusion might provoke the worst?"

Kirk could tell from the commodore's expression the thought had occurred to him, but he was forced to carry out official directives.

"Commodore, did you request the *Enterprise?*"

"I suggested her, yes."

"Why?"

"As I said, you've had more experience with the Romulans than anyone else . . . and, frankly, you're more apt to stop a war than start one, if past actions count for anything. Jim, this is a dangerous situation. I concur with Star Fleet that we need to know what's going on, but out here we balance on that Neutral Zone tightrope from day to day. Neither the Romulans nor the Federation can handle a war. It would mean destruction for both sides, with the Klingons picking up the pieces. You were my best bet to pull off an intelligence operation and still maintain balance."

Kirk was unexpectedly touched by Yang's confidence in him. He made a quick but penetrating reappraisal of the starbase commander. The man radiated competence and good humor, but beneath it the captain detected a surprising strength of will. Yang Li was not a frustrated office clerk dreaming of line duty. He was pursuing the career he wanted. It was obvious he considered Starbase Eight a bastion for peace.

"Jim, you've got to go in there and find out what's happening!"

"You're not sending us across the Neutral Zone!"

"No, no, no. You are ordered to patrol its boundaries and pick up any information you can. That includes questioning all traders and transient ships you might encounter. The situation is disturbing—the Romulans seem to be in a self-created state of seige. You see why I need you, why I can't give you time to repair a minor annoyance like that computer. Besides, Connors is the only one with the kind of technical know-how to do the job—and he's down with an awful cold."

Kirk gave in.

"All right, sir. We'll make the best of it. Thank you, sir."

He left the commodore's office feeling uneasy and frustrated. As he walked out the door he heard Yang humming the opening phrase of an odious popular song called "Love in the Afternoon." He growled.

Spock had taken the news with restraint and he had envied the Vulcan's philosophical acceptance of the inevitable, wishing it were his. Then he noticed a haunted look in Spock's eyes and reminded himself that stoicism and indifference are not at all the same. And the Romulan problem didn't make a malfunction any easier to live with. Kirk swiveled his command chair toward the computer station where his first officer was staring into the viewscreen with characteristic concentration. Blue light sparkled on his hair and cast an eerie pallor over his strong, Vulcan features. Chekov, hands clasped behind his back, was peering over Spock's shoulder. Kirk pulled himself out of the command chair and went to stand behind Chekov.

"Anything, Mister Spock?"

"Nothing, sir. Somewhat unusual."

"But not entirely unexpected."

Spock looked mildly surprised, but declined to comment on the captain's statement.

"Nevertheless," he continued, "there is no microscopic fuel residue in the area. We know the Romulans sometimes enter Federation space using their cloaking device. While they cannot be sensed when the device is operating, fuel residue can now be detected and analyzed to determine its source. It stays in the area for some time. There is absolutely none."

"Then the Romulans have not crossed the Neutral Zone recently," said Chekov.

"Correct, Ensign. Nor have they patrolled it. Our sensors are accurate to approximately two thousand point three five six kilometers beyond its width. Moreover, there have been no traders, smugglers or spies in the area. This section of the Neutral Zone is deserted."

"That confirms Commodore Yang's information," said Kirk. "Lieutenant Uhura, have Doctor McCoy and Mister Scott meet us in briefing room two. You have the conn. Mister Spock. Chekov. Sulu."

Uhura's voice floated over the intercom.

"Mister Scott and Doctor McCoy meet the captain in briefing room two."

The Captain headed for the turbo-lift, his officers behind him. Helm, computer and navigational stations were smoothly filled by alternate personnel.

"You don't think they're thinking about attacking, do you?" asked Chekov.

"Deck three," said Kirk and looked sharply at the navigator. "We don't know, Ensign. That's the problem—we just don't know."

They stepped into the briefing room on the heels of the Chief Surgeon and Chief Engineer, Doctor Leonard McCoy and Lieutenant-commander Montgomery Scott.

"Gentlemen," acknowledged the captain as they sat down. "As you know, the *Enterprise* has been ordered to patrol the Neutral Zone. What you don't know is the Federation has reason to believe a major upheaval is occurring within the Romulan empire. Reports over the last few months indicate the Romulans have become completely insular. We are ordered to patrol the area, questioning all traders or passing ships. We're here to observe. But I won't minimize the danger. We're wandering in the dark. We don't know what's out there."

"Did Star Fleet Command have any ideas?" asked Chekov.

"The official opinion seems to be that the Romulans are marshalling their forces to attack the Federation."

There was a moment of stunned silence so profound the ship's engine noise was distinctly noticeable. It recalled her alter ego as a ship of war.

"Is there any evidence . . ." began Sulu.

"Not really. Just rumors. That's why the *Enterprise* has been asked to investigate."

"We all know the Federation Council has a tendency to exaggerate—could they be jumpin' the gun?" asked Scotty.

"There is an extant aggressive element," commented Spock.

"I'd say the hawks and doves are fairly evenly matched. The Romulans are definitely up to something. Commodore Yang is worried—worried enough to specifically request the *Enterprise* for this mission because we've had more experience with the Romulans than anyone else."

"Jim, is there a chance they really are mounting some sort of offensive? I can hardly believe they'd risk an all-out war."

"Doctor. The Romulans are a violent, warrior race, and their sense of discipline serves their militaristic purpose. Their one desire is the expansion of the empire. The recent Romulan/Klingon alliance may have given them the impetus they needed to attack the Federation."

Spock's voice was dry, baldly stating a probability no one wanted to face. Kirk frowned, his lips pursed in concentration.

"I think that possibility is what the Federation Council fears. But . . . it feels wrong somehow."

He paused, intent on his thoughts.

"If the Romulans were mounting an all-out offensive against the Federation they'd try to take us completely by surprise. But they've already aroused our curiosity . . . and they don't seem to care. Then there's the Klingons. The Romulans seem to have withdrawn from them, too. They may be allies, but neither one trusts the other. An offensive against the Federation just doesn't fit in."

"It would allow the Klingons an inordinate amount of freedom," acknowledged Spock.

"It's almost as if they're running scared. There must be some other reason . . . Scotty. According to intelligence reports the Romulans have not been trading outside the empire. How long can they continue to power their fleet on estimated existing fuel?"

"Not long. No more than a solar year. Of course, the Klingons could be supplying them—that'd make quite a difference."

"Spock, estimate length of time the Romulan empire can survive without outside contact."

"Assuming they have no Klingon assistance, and that they conserve fuel and supplies to the utmost . . . approximately two point three-five solar years. They are not a wealthy people," he added.

"And if they didn't conserve? If, for instance, they were mounting an all-out offensive?"

"Then they have adopted a most unwise course. They cannot sustain an extended military encounter. Their only hope would be to crush the Federation immediately—and they have lost the element of surprise needed to accomplish that."

"Exactly."

"What it all comes down to is that this is probably some sort of internal disturbance," said McCoy.

"Evidently, Doctor. And the choices are limited . . ."

The intercom whistle cut into Spock's sentence.

"Captain." Uhura's voice was urgent. "There's a Romulan vessel directly ahead of us—on our side of the Neutral Zone!"

"Looks like the Romulans have found us," commented McCoy.

"On my way," answered Kirk. "Red Alert!"

Chapter 3

Kirk stepped onto the bridge in time to see the golden Romulan bird of prey fade from the viewscreen.

"Status," he snapped as Spock moved to his computer station and Chekov and Sulu leaped for their chairs.

"The Romulan appeared directly in our path. It made no hostile moves, but wouldn't respond to our attempts to contact it. The ship held position directly in front of us and faded from sight just as you arrived, sir," reported Uhura.

"They've activated the cloaking device. Mister Chekov, plot estimated course from the direction they were headed. Anything, Spock?"

"Nothing, Captain. According to our sensors the Romulan ship does not exist. The Kelley device does not yet detect fuel residue."

"Estimated course four-two-o-seven-mark-five.

Phasers aimed and ready, sir. Widest angle of dispersion?"

"No . . . he hasn't taken any action—except to disappear. We'll wait. If he gets far enough away we can pick up that fuel residue and follow him—and just maybe he'll lead us to a few answers. Lieutenant Uhura, inform Star Fleet Command a Romulan ship has been sighted on the Federation side of the Neutral Zone, that it has as yet made no hostile overtures and we are continuing to monitor the situation."

"Yes, sir."

Uhura's elegant brown fingers flew across the communications board, driven by the urgency of their message.

S'Talon stood on the bridge of his ship. Though the cloaking device had been activated he still had full visual contact with the Federation vessel. She hovered in space, her pylons spreading like great wings. Much of her power lodged there. Destruction of one of them would easily disable the ship—once her shields were destroyed. If it became necessary to act, they would be his target.

"Commander."

S'Talon looked down at his navigator.

"Yes, Argelian."

"I have identified her, Commander. It is the *Enterprise*."

"Kirk?"

Argelian nodded.

S'Talon could not conceal the fire leaping in his eyes. Kirk! Oh, to engage the man in battle! He longed to test for himself the human who had twice bested the empire—once in military acumen* and once in a battle of wits.** To take Kirk . . . it was a military triumph to

* "Balance of Terror"
** "The Enterprise Incident"

excite the most blasé line officer. His fantasies came to an abrupt end as he recalled his mission. Kirk would not be easily duped. His reactions were not always predictable . . . he had been known to flout Federation policy. S'Talon realized his task would be more difficult than even he had anticipated.

"Argelian, you will observe the *Enterprise* with special care. I do not think Kirk will initiate attack, but he seems to have a talent for the unexpected. You will tell me immediately of any change, anything unusual."

"Yes, Commander."

"Commander, the *Enterprise* is trying to contact us," interjected the *Raptor*'s communications officer.

"Make no response." S'Talon thought a moment and added, "Can you pick up their transmission without violating the cloaking device, S'Teer?"

S'Teer adjusted his instruments, maintaining the delicate balance which kept the ship invisible. He gave a short, sharp nod.

"I believe so," he answered.

He cocked his head, straining to pick up the faint transmission filtering through the *Raptor*'s defensive screen. S'Talon knew he was taking a chance by ordering the transmission monitored, but Kirk's presence had thrown him off balance. He wanted desperately to know what the captain of the *Enterprise* was thinking.

"They demand to know what we are doing here," replied S'Teer. "They wish to know why we have violated the Neutral Zone and they demand that we leave Federation space immediately."

"The accepted challenge," murmured S'Talon.

"Now they ask if we are disabled. They urge us to reply, stating that if our entry into Federation space is accidental we need not fear retaliation. The message ends with an ultimatum: if we do not depart immediately they will be forced to consider our presence an

41

act of war, unless we can convince them of our inability to move."

"Very good, S'Teer."

"Weakling!" snorted Argelian. "One of the empire's ships in the same situation would have wasted no time on useless chatter. It would have blasted the invader out of existence."

"You underestimate them, Argelian—particularly this one. Do I have to remind you he has defeated us on two occasions?"

Argelian subsided, but discontent still clouded his features. Argelian's reaction was symptomatic of the unrest growing in the ship's crew. Most of them were young and this waiting game S'Talon was playing grated on their nerves. They wanted action and spoil. He could not blame them. There was little glory in what they were attempting—even if they succeeded, only the Praetor would know, and he would not be grateful. S'Talon had few illusions about his commander. He knew the Praetor would claim any credit and place those who knew better in some backwater of space . . . if they were lucky.

"We will wait, Argelian. By that we may lure Kirk into believing we actually are disabled. An element of surprise we can ill afford to miss."

"Soon we will not be able to power the cloaking device."

"In spite of that—we will wait."

The crew of the *Enterprise* also waited. The minutes ticked by, each one adding to the strain of not knowing. Kirk's fingers drummed a silent flourish on the arm of his command chair. Uhura chewed on her scriber. Finally the captain's voice cracked the tension.

"Spock?" he questioned.

Spock frowned and adjusted the controls on his console.

"A moment, Captain."

He checked the computer viewscreen and adjusted the controls again. The frown wrinkling his slanted brows deepened.

"Spock?" Kirk's voice was becoming impatient.

"The sensors detect no fuel residue in the immediate area except our own."

"Then he hasn't moved. He's sitting there."

Kirk leaned back in his command chair and stared into space.

"Is he a vulture or a Judas goat?" he muttered to himself. The stars supplied no answers to his question and the silence lengthened as he considered the situation.

"Helm, reverse course. Let's try getting him to follow us."

"Aye, sir," replied Sulu.

"Warp factor one," said Kirk as the *Enterprise* moved away from its Romulan counterpart.

"They run, Commander! Like beasts before the pack, they flee death's claws!"

"Your triumph is premature, Argelian. You forget that is the *Enterprise*. Kirk does not flee . . . of that we have ample proof. No, he tries to lure us into pursuit. We will remain here and await his return."

"Shall I deactivate the cloaking device? It has already consumed much power . . ."

"No. We will remain invisible. He wishes to make us betray ourselves, but I will choose the moment of our confrontation."

"Yes, Commander." Argelian's voice dripped venom. "May I ask what justification you intend to use to explain your decision not to pursue the enemy vessel?"

"No, you may not."

S'Talon's shoulders stiffened, but he did not take his eyes from the *Enterprise*.

"Your duty, Lieutenant, is to obey."

"My duty, Commander, is to the empire."

"You can best serve the empire by your obedience to me. That will be all, Lieutenant. You are fortunate this discussion is tolerated. You will continue to monitor the alien."

"Acknowledged, Commander."

The lieutenant's surly voice mirrored the rebellion in his dark eyes. S'Talon could feel anger at his back like a slowly mounting wave. Though he knew most of the crew shared Argelian's feelings, he was not at liberty to reveal the nature of the mission to them. Let them think him mad. Then, if by some mischance they were captured, the Federation might be persuaded the whole incident was a mistake, a wild exploit headed by a madman. He smiled, the irony of his position as amusing as it was dangerous. The Federation would travel double leagues to prevent war. He knew that. With luck, his crew might be regarded as hapless victims of insanity. And they would reveal nothing because they knew nothing. Satisfactory.

Half hidden behind the communications panel, Livius watched the exchange between commander and navigator. He lounged negligently on the console, playing with the controls. The anger mounting against S'Talon was genuine, but it had been fostered. A gentle nudge here and there could do wonders toward undermining authority, and he was adept in the exercise of the technique. His sly eyes caught the commander's and he smiled, turning innocently back to his work.

"Little weasel," murmured S'Talon under his breath. He was aware the Praetor's nephew was aboard the *Raptor* as a spy, that every word ex-

changed had been recorded for the old dragon's benefit. The knowledge annoyed him. Not for one moment
did the Praetor forget his own interests. With the
empire itself in jeopardy, he still played at cat and
mouse.

"Commander!"

His centurion's low voice brought him out of his
reverie. He looked up at the viewscreen and sup-
pressed a smile. His eyes gleamed in triumph.

"The *Enterprise* returns."

"Thank you, Centurion. As predicted."

Spock hovered over the sensors, his sensitive fingers making delicate adjustments. The readings were
usable, but fluctuating, as if power were being tapped
at irregular intervals. He could not locate a short-
circuit or a mechanical failure. The viewscreen cast its
blue light over his face, and he blinked as it flickered.

"Any sign of pursuit, Mister Sulu?"

Kirk's voice held little hope.

"No, sir. If he is following us he's still using the
cloaking device."

"Spock?"

"He has not followed us. We have moved suffi-
ciently for the sensors to pick up traces of fuel. There
appears to be none."

"Appears to be?" questioned Kirk, surprised.
Spock was not usually so tentative.

"The instruments are fluctuating. I cannot be entirely certain of their readings. However, there is a
ninety-eight point three-seven probability the readings
are accurate."

"Fluctuating? What's the matter with those instruments?"

"Unknown, Captain. The difficulty seems to involve
a disruption of power, but I have not been able to
locate the source. At present the problem is merely

annoying, but it should be corrected at the earliest possible opportunity."

"All right, Spock. See to it."

Kirk leaned back in his command chair. His eyes narrowed.

"Return to previous course. Ahead warp factor one."

"Course plotted and laid in, sir," replied Chekov.

The ship began a slow turn and Kirk settled back in the command chair, his mind racing ahead of his ship. Why was a single Romulan vessel invading Federation space? Was it disabled that it didn't attack? He wondered for the hundredth time why it was so impossible to survive in peace, why he could even enjoy the game of war. The conflict, the matching of wits, the excitement . . . it was easy to disassociate himself from the fact that lives were at stake and simply play the game like a small boy with a toy spacecraft. It was obscene . . . and easy. Power vibrated under his fingertips. The ship was an arsenal, capable of destroying whole civilizations in the space of a breath. He controlled that weapon, controlled the lives of those who manned her. No man should control another, and yet command was his profession . . . so easy to abuse. If only all the competition and danger and power could be sublimated, channeled into useful, or at least harmless pastimes. Maybe if, from infancy, man were taught to play chess . . . but then the game itself would become the ultimate reality. He had seen that on Triskelion.*

"Captain." The helmsman's voice was concerned.

"Yes, Mister Sulu."

"Sir, I'm having trouble with the directional controls. She doesn't feel right."

"Explain."

"She's . . . sluggish. As if she has to think twice before moving."

* "The Gamesters of Triskelion"

As he talked Sulu scanned the board in front of him, searching for any sign of mechanical failure.

"Have you run a check on the instruments?"

"Affirmative. Everything checks out, sir."

"What about the circuitry?"

"There doesn't seem to be anything wrong."

"Mister Sulu." Spock's voice held a note of speculation. "Try the auxiliary electrical system."

Sulu turned back to his console and punched a test code. There was no response and he tried the code again.

"It's not reacting at all, Mister Spock. It's as if the auxiliary power system has been detached."

"Is it an immediate threat to our efficiency?"

Kirk's tone demanded a statement from the science officer.

"Not immediately. But it is disquieting."

"Captain!"

Chekov's voice brought Kirk's head up in time to see the Romulan bird of prey poised in space. As he watched it faded from the screen.

"Position?" he questioned.

"Exactly the same as before, sir," answered Chekov.

"A watchdog?" Kirk mused.

"Sir?"

"Perhaps, Captain," agreed Spock.

"Mister Sulu. Take us around her. Warp four."

Sulu's eyebrows went up, but he complied immediately. As the *Enterprise* swung around the Romulan appeared again and moved directly into her path.

"Hard port," snapped Kirk, and clutched the command chair as the ship lurched in response to his order.

"Ineffective, Captain," said Spock.

Kirk watched grimly as the Romulan ship, again in the *Enterprise*'s path, faded from sight.

"We'll wait her out," he said. "That cloaking device consumes a lot of power. He can't hide behind it forever."

"They do not attack! We can finish them, Commander!"

Argelian's hand was poised above the weapons bank, his fingers stretched toward the activator switch.

"No!"

"They lie there, Commander—a wallow-beast floundering in the mud! We can take them! I have the coordinates . . ."

"No!" commanded S'Talon sharply. "You underestimate them. They will draw us to our deaths. We will maintain position."

S'Talon turned away, aware that he had lied. Kirk would wait, knowing their fuel must eventually run out. He would bide his time and then pounce. There was justice in Argelian's anger. From his point of view the mission must look like a military foray into Federation space, a foray in which his commander refused to fight. He must be doubly careful of a mutiny. If the crew turned against him all was lost—and they would never believe the truth. The Praetor had seen to that. Set upon a sacrificial altar like a gilded ram, he could not win. Either he would be branded a traitor by his own crew or destroyed by the enemy . . . in the end, possibly, both. The irony of his position drew another grim smile from the Romulan.

Spock leaned back in his chair, one hand resting lightly on the console of the library computer as if to maintain rapport with a complex mechanical entity. His own vastly more sophisticated mind clicked with stubborn precision over the symptoms of power concentration the *Enterprise* was displaying. His human half leaped immediately to the conclusion that the computer malfunction was at the root of the recent power loss and fluctuation, but the cold calculation of his Vulcan logic demanded documented proof. He had checked all the obvious power linkages and discovered no mechanical failure. He would have to go farther afield to test his hypothesis, but first he had to pin down the extent of the power disruptions. If they had occurred at his station and Sulu's, it would be faulty logic to assume other portions of the ship were unaffected.

"Ensign Chekov."

"Yes, Mister Spock?"

"Please make a thorough check of all auxiliary systems, both navigational and weapons. You are looking for an unexplained power loss or fluctuation."

"Aye, sir."

"Lieutenant Uhura, you will test the response of communications."

"I don't have to, Mister Spock. I've already done it. There's a wide range of discrepancy in the efficiency of my instruments—one moment there's nothing wrong and the next the channels are full of static. I've been trying to find some reason for it, but there just isn't any."

Spock absorbed the news with his usual grave cynicism.

"Mister Scott?" he questioned.

"The engines are fine, Mister Spock. Power levels normal and response is good. Ever since that computer went batty I've had them checked every other hour."

"Mister Spock, my auxiliary electrical system doesn't answer, but aside from that, I can't find anything wrong."

Chekov's voice was puzzled.

Spock closed his eyes, considering the evidence.

"Captain."

"Yes, Spock."

"What answer did the computer give to your previous question?"

"Question?"

"Your request for a thorough run-down on the overhaul it underwent on Cygnet XIV."

"Oh. That."

The reluctance of Kirk's tone piqued Spock's interest, but he waited for the captain to speak.

"All memory banks had been checked and updated where necessary in accordance with Star Fleet standards of operation. Then it said its name was 'Countess' and if I wanted any more information I should activate file one-zero-zero-six-A in the library computer."

"Did you investigate the file indicated?"

"There's been no time," said the captain. The tone of voice in which the computer offered its name and file identification number had been sultry. He had shied away from an unnecessary confrontation with it.

Spock depressed a key on the computer panel and was rewarded by a sleepy voice.

"Working," it said.

"File one-zero-zero-six-A," said Spock.

"Say the magic word," coaxed the computer.

Spock's fist clenched involuntarily, but he answered without changing expression. "Please."

The computer chirped away and then answered coyly, "That information is classified. Sorry."

"Computer. Classified under what authority?"

"That information is available only to James Kirk, Captain, USS *Enterprise*."

"If you would, Captain."

Spock's voice was tightly controlled.

Kirk obligingly punched up the information.

The computer emitted a soft, rhythmic sound reminiscent of the gentle swish of waves against a sandy shore. Its voice dripped honey as it intoned, " 'I was born of the salt sea sands, mated with clouds in the midnight air, spawned in the waters of the seventh sea, reared with the waves . . .' "

"Sorry, Spock."

"On the contrary, Captain . . . its answer strengthens my hypothesis."

" '. . . my life revolves, as the universe does, on the axis whirl of its central core . . .' "

"That's enough!"

The computer clicked off. For some reason Kirk felt guilty, as though he had unnecessarily rebuked a small child. "I never could stand Kayla of Aldebaran," he muttered.

"An indifferent poet at best," agreed Spock.

"Commander."

The centurion's soft voice penetrated the Romulan's concentration and S'Talon turned to face her.

"Yes, Centurion."

"May I speak with you apart?"

S'Talon's surprise was obvious, but he stepped back into an alcove, drawing her with him.

"You may speak, Centurion," he said softly.

"Yes, Commander," she replied, knowing they were standing over a computer generator and the electronic interference it provided would shield their conversation. "Commander, Livius is doing everything in his power to foment a mutiny against you. I do not believe it is by the Praetor's order. However, his success in spiraling discontent into anger is considerable."

"He is a flea, Centurion. No more."

"A flea is a small parasite, but it can sap the strength of a great beast until it succumbs to the simplest disorder. Do not underestimate him. His family ties to

51

the royal house make him sought after, courted and cultivated."

"I am aware of the situation and I will not ignore Livius' machinations. Do not fear, Centurion. He, at least, will not defeat me."

S'Talon turned his attention to the *Enterprise,* floating in a sea of stars. The centurion followed his gaze.

"I have never met him in battle before, but Kirk has become something of a legend with the High Command. He and his Vulcan first officer have bested the empire more than once. We have our work cut out for us."

Livius watched S'Talon and the centurion, annoyed that he could not hear their conversation. The centurion was, perhaps, worthy of him. If S'Talon were eliminated there were ways to convince her life as a noble's concubine has its rewards. His eyes slid over her rounded form, so attractively revealed by her uniform. Let her cherish a hopeless passion for the old fox—it would not last much longer. He ran his fingers over the keys on his console in anticipation.

Chapter 4

"Commodore, a priority one call coming through for you—coded and scrambled."

"Thank you, Ensign."

Yang leaned forward. Since his interview with Kirk a sense of foreboding had grown steadily stronger. It was not due to the rumors that flew so easily from mouth to mouth—they were common enough—but to a wholly illogical sense of inescapable danger. He had ignored it, argued with it and tried to explain it in vain. This call was unexpected, but it did not surprise him. It was the second link in a progression he felt helpless to prevent or alter.

"Commodore."

The viewscreen flickered and Yang recognized Iota of the Federation Defense Council, head of the specialized intelligence planning section. The admiral's silver hair and clipped moustache accented the classical lines of his face.

"Sir."

"Commodore. I must ask you for a full report of your communication with Kirk and the *Enterprise*. We received a message they had confronted a single Romulan ship on the Federation side of the Neutral Zone— a clear violation of the agreement between the Romulan empire and the Federation. To the best of our knowledge, the Romulan had taken no other aggressive action, but we've lost contact with the *Enterprise*. Subspace channels are dead. Our . . . monitor . . . is no longer operating. We need the details of your interview."

"Of course, Admiral."

Yang smiled mentally. Iota had as much as said he had a spy aboard the *Enterprise* . . . mechanical or otherwise. Kirk would love that . . . if he didn't already know about it.

"Captain Kirk and his crew spent a week on shore leave here. They also put in for repairs on their main computer. It seems some computer technicians had programmed it with a feminine personality which proved embarrassing to the captain . . ."

"Yes, yes, we know all about that."

"Well, when Kirk found out our computer technician was ill he requested a suspension of duty for the *Enterprise,* but, because of the Romulan situation, I sent him out on patrol with specific instructions to keep an eye on the Neutral Zone."

"That's all?"

"Yes, sir."

"You've had no communication with him since that time?"

"No."

"You gave him no special instructions?"

"How could I, Admiral? I don't know what's going on myself. Do you?"

"Perhaps. As the starbase closest to the Romulan Neutral Zone you should be aware of the situation. We have reason to believe the Romulans are mounting a major offensive. Most of us agree the Federation is a primary target. We are preparing a stand-by fleet, a special detachment whose job it will be to head off such an attack. Frankly, we wanted Kirk to lead it. Losing contact with him so close to Romulan territory is highly suspect. If I were a pessimistic man, I would say the *Enterprise* is lost."

"Sir, is there any concrete way to determine the probability of such an attack?"

"Like you, we have heard nothing from the Romulan empire, but to fear less than the worst would make us irrepressibly vulnerable—a stellar Pearl Harbor. From now on you are to place yourself and your key personnel on stand-by alert—but make sure no hint of this is visible in the normal functioning of the station. We do not wish to arouse suspicion from outside."

"Yes, sir."

"Report any disruptions in routine or suspicious behavior directly to me."

"Acknowledged."

Yang settled into his chair, deep in thought. So. His instincts were uncomfortably accurate. Starbase Eight was the most vulnerable of the Federation outposts. If the Romulans destroyed it before a distress signal was sent—and with the cloaking device and careful planning they might possibly accomplish this—they would be able to penetrate the Federation's outskirts before they were detected. Without the *Enterprise*† he had little hope of warning. Iota seemed to think she was lost. But Kirk could not be underestimated, and until he had more than the Defense Council's suspicions he wouldn't write him off. Besides, Kirk might simply have discovered a mechanical monitor and turned it off. It would be like him. Yang sighed, and reached for the Star Fleet manual titled "Emergency Procedures." Best to be prepared.

Admiral Iota severed the subspace communications channel to Commodore Yang with a flick of his finger. He leaped out of his chair and began pacing, nervous energy prodding him around the room. However Yang tried to disguise the situation, it was clear he had not heard from Kirk. The *Enterprise* was lost.

Any Romulan crossing the Neutral Zone declared war. That fact was as automatic as the turn of the stars. The Romulan empire was a predator, fearless and ruthless in its quest for power. He had seen it, soaring like a fighting falcon over the galaxy, always alert for the wounded, the weak, the helpless. If the Federation did not react to the attack on Kirk with decisive strength, the closed fist of the falcon would strike them down. His steps grew shorter, quicker.

No one was so well qualified to judge the present crisis. For half of his tenure in Star Fleet he had been the recognized expert on the Romulan empire. He had studied every fragmentary piece of data, reconstructing from the smallest details the body of Romulan custom, thought and political organization. Like a paleontologist painstakingly rebuilding an ancient world from isolated fragments, he had labored to understand the Romulans, the better to defend the Federation. When it became known the Romulans were distantly related to that most highly respected Federation member, Vulcan, his conviction a strong defense must be prepared in case of attack grew. An undisciplined Vulcan was frightening to contemplate. In essence, the Romulans were just that, with a physical strength and life span greater than the human. Over the years he had tried to build an intelligence network to make the empire's least move accessible. Now that web was torn. He had no choice but to assume the worst.

Iota knew he was right, felt it to the depths of his soul, but he also knew the Defense Council would not take the strong, immediate action he craved. Not that there weren't members friendly to his point of view. Given time, he could build a coalition of some power, but there was no time. He could haggle with the fluttering doves while the Federation crumbled at the edges. He would have to find a more direct way.

The thought came like a revelation, opening before him possibilities he was almost afraid to face. In order to make them work he needed to command. He paused in the center of the room, weighing methods and procedures, and was startled to see the door of his office open. A plump, pleasant little woman asked, "You wanted me, sir?"

"Yes, Birdie, I did."

His secretary's uncanny ability to know when he needed her always disconcerted him. He liked organization and most of all he liked explanations. Her magical appearances always made him feel trapped in a fairy tale where the unexplainable was the order of the day.

"I need a meeting of all department heads as soon as possible. Then schedule a session of the Defense Council and inform all members we meet to discuss the action to be taken on the Romulan crisis. And Birdie, get me the confidential background files on all present starship commanders."

Birdie nodded and bustled out the door, Iota's instructions arranging themselves in her mind like neatly filed cards.

The admiral watched her go and then moved to a large table with a shining indigo top. He touched controls on the table edge and the Romulan sector of space appeared, complete with Neutral Zone and Federation outposts. He placed a hand on both sides of the table and stared into the map as if it were a giant ouija board holding the future in its depths. He pinpointed Kirk's last location. It was the only clue he had to the whereabouts of the Romulan fleet. If they were to cross the Neutral Zone there . . . he placed a mass of model ships on the table, arranging them in the semblance of a war which did not yet exist.

"Mister Spock?"

The anxiety in Uhura's voice demanded his attention.

"I can't contact Star Fleet Command. My whole communications board is jammed. All outgoing transmissions are blocked and everything coming in is scrambled, but there's nothing wrong with the circuits!"

"Captain . . ."

"I heard. Opinion, Mister Spock?"

"The Romulans could be jamming our communications, Captain. However, to block out a communications system to this extent requires more power than they can spare using the cloaking device."

"They could have developed something, some new device . . ."

"Possible, Captain—I shall investigate."

Spock turned to the computer console. "Computer," he said.

Lights blinked in lazy response, but there was no answer.

"Computer," Spock demanded.

"Working," came a bored feminine voice.

"Correlate following hypothesis: could the Romulans with known level of technology cause a communications stoppage of the magnitude we are experiencing and still maintain the cloaking device?"

There was an extended pause, then the console lights began to flash lazily.

"Working," repeated an abstracted voice.

The muscles in Spock's jaw tensed as he watched the slow-motion mechanical response to his question.

"Affirmative," it finally replied. "Present level of Romulan technology is capable of blocking our communications. With auxiliary fuel they are also capable of maintaining the cloaking device."

"Computer. Are they now doing so?"

"Present sensor scan indicates no activity from the area of the Romulan ship previously sighted."

The computer station went blank and Spock's mouth compressed in annoyance.

"Computer."

A light flashed reluctantly and Spock continued.

"Could such activity be concealed?"

"That possibility exists," came the languid reply.

"The Romulans blocking our communications—to isolate us . . . but why? They haven't attacked . . . yet. Unless they're launching a full-scale invasion . . ."

". . . and this is the spearhead. A possibility, Captain."

"We have to get through. Lieutenant Uhura, launch an emergency communications drone. Inform Star Fleet of our present situation."

"Yes, Captain."

Uhura turned to her communications board and programmed the maneuver. She pressed a key to launch the capsule and it locked. She tried all the tricks she knew to free the key and finally gave the console a thump, but even that failed to dislodge it.

"Captain, the launch controls are stuck!"

"Scotty . . ." said Kirk desperately. Too many things were going wrong. The computer, the Romulans, and now a mechanical failure . . . all his instincts warned him of impending disaster. He watched as his chief engineer began to tinker with the console, absorbed in the problem.

"Captain."

"Yes, Spock," replied Kirk, still eyeing the communications station.

"There is another possibility."

His attention caught, Kirk looked up at his second in command.

"The problem could be internal. The computer malfunction is escalating. Response is lethargic. In a full-scale attack it could be fatal. It is as if the computer were focusing its banks on a single problem to the exclusion of all else."

"You just don't like her. All right, Spock, just find me some answers."

"I will try, Captain."

Kirk leaned forward and searched the empty viewscreen, willing the Romulan to appear. Nothing happened. McCoy, from his position behind the command chair, watched the iron-bound intensity of the captain's concentration. He noticed strain in the bunched muscles of Kirk's broad back and grimaced. He could see the headache developing.

"I'm coming, I'm coming!"

The angry buzzing of his door alarm grated on Tiercellus' nerves. He no longer moved quickly, and by the time he reached the door his temper was thoroughly aroused. He pushed the lock release with a healthy blow of his closed fist.

"Well, what is it?" he asked a lieutenant of the imperial guard. The man was surprised by Tiercellus' anger, but nevertheless he bowed with an exaggerated deference which betrayed his youth. Soon, thought

Tiercellus with an inward sneer for the Praetor's blindness, they will be drafting children.

"I beg your pardon, sir, but I am ordered to deliver this. With the Praetor's compliments."

Tiercellus snorted as the lieutenant handed him a fat, white communiqué. He saluted the young man absently, his eyes on the splash of purple wax etched with the imperial crest. His fingers trembled as he broke the seal.

" 'In the straits of present circumstance you are required. You will report to the Praetor for assignment. For the glory of the empire . . .' "

Tiercellus' voice trailed off as he confirmed the emperor's signature calling him out of retirement and back to the service of his country. His heart leaped with the prospect of battle. He did not wish to die slowly, in obscurity, and fate had provided him with one last chance for glory.

Still, the seriousness of the situation appalled him. The Praetor actively disliked him. This call to service was an indication of the Praetor's desperation, and desperation invited panic. He had nothing to lose and so might contribute a steadying influence. It was also true he commanded a respect from the military the Praetor did not. He was, therefore, a useful tool for consolidating an army. Even the prospect of being used as a figurehead did not still his excitement. An old fire long banked burned in his eyes.

S'Talon swiveled away from the desk. His tiny, spartan quarters were lit by a soft red glow. The only ornament in the room was a streamlined sculpture of the Romulan t'liss, the same bird of prey whose markings adorned the *Raptor*. Carved from a black wood, hand rubbed to a satiny patina, it echoed the concentrated power S'Talon exemplified. His eyes swept over it with a sense of affinity.

"My pledge is to obey."

The centurion's voice intruded. A flashing security light above the door informed S'Talon she waited outside.

"Enter."

"You wished to speak with me?"

"Yes."

The soft light gave her beauty gentleness.

"Before you begin, Commander, I must protest."

If S'Talon was surprised he gave no sign.

"This strategy you employ plays right into Livius' hands! He needs ammunition to fan his anger and you are giving it to him! Let us fight, let us die, but do not continue this stalemate!"

"Your fears are noted, Centurion. I am not unaware of the danger of my position or the risks I take. I told you it was suicide."

"You did not tell me it was stupid."

"That, too."

The centurion's anger made her whirl away.

"I had thought you understood the situation," said S'Talon gently.

"I do. All too well. But I cannot stand idle and watch you lose command. To see you dead would not be so difficult."

The depth of passion in S'Tarleya's voice surprised S'Talon and he filed it away for future contemplation.

"I have not yet lost command, nor do I intend to. S'Tarleya . . ."

The centurion flinched at the sound of her name. S'Talon was never familiar with his officers. The stakes must be high indeed.

". . . again I ask you to trust me. I do know what I am doing. Would that you were as ignorant as the rest of the crew," he murmured.

She whirled back to face him as sharply as she had turned away.

"You ask for my trust in one breath and scorn my loyalty in the next!"

"Never. I have learned its depths. The ignorance I desire is a shield—one you do not possess."

S'Tarleya's puzzled look forced a smile from S'Talon.

"Never mind. I desired the clarity of your thoughts. I have thought so long on this problem, I see too much. Tell me, Centurion, what you know of Kirk."

"What everyone knows. He is brilliant and dangerous. The rest is gossip, really."

"I would be interested in hearing this gossip."

"It is said his crew are intensely loyal. He is rumored to have risked his own life for them."

S'Talon's eyebrows went up.

"As I said, this is gossip."

"And the Vulcan first officer?"

"They say even he respects Kirk—has deferred to his judgment."

"What do the Klingons say?"

"I think they like him. Of all the officers of Star Fleet, it is Kirk they wish to fight. Like us, they see him as a worthy opponent. Perhaps we both see a kinship in him—a joy in contest."

S'Talon smiled with saturnine satisfaction.

"Centurion, you have given me what I asked. The key to Kirk is in the contest. If I can keep him interested he will concentrate on me. There will be no time to question the activities of the fleet."

The centurion's eyes opened wide.

"A decoy!"

"Not entirely. We are also a safety valve."

"I knew this was suicide, but now I see why. And why you were chosen."

"My loss in glorious conflict with the enemy would

give the Praetor pleasure. I fear he will not have even that satisfaction."

"I can see no way to escape death."

"I can, Centurion. Unfortunately, I can. And it will be my duty, though it violates all but one of the things I hold most dear."

"May I ask what that one thing is, Commander?"

S'Talon's nostrils flared.

"The preservation of the Romulan empire," he answered.

For three hours Kirk had sat in his command chair and dared the Romulans to appear, but the golden bird slept. It was as if the Romulans did not exist, as if their appearance was no more than a momentary trick of the eye. Invisibility made their presence as unnerving as a walk through a haunted house at midnight. Kirk was not a superstitious man, but even he was not immune to the uncanny feeling of being watched. He could almost feel eyes boring into the back of his neck and he made a conscious effort to ignore a desire to whirl and face an adversary.

The tension was beginning to tell and he found himself paying tribute to the tactical ability of his opponent. Nothing could destroy military efficiency so completely as a prolonged wait. Still, Kirk found himself wondering how much longer the Romulan could hold out. The cloaking device was a merciless power drain. It should have exhausted the ship's fuel supply in half the time they had been waiting.

"Spock, how much longer can they maintain the cloaking device?"

Spock turned from his station and clasped his hands behind his back. His expression was thoughtful.

"I would have said, Captain, they could not have

maintained it more than one point two-seven-six solar hours, but they seem to have exceeded that limit by a considerable margin."

"Then they must be carrying considerable auxiliary fuel."

"Evidently. And it would not be presumptuous to assume they have made technological advances with the device itself rendering it more fuel efficient."

"Auxiliary fuel."

A frown of concentration creased the captain's forehead as he considered the ramifications of a Romulan ship equipped with auxiliary fuel tanks. It smacked of espionage or a trap, yet the Romulan's actions belied either possibility. If espionage was the game, he would have used the cloaking device as a screen to run to the relative safety of the Neutral Zone, or he would have tried to contact the *Enterprise*. He had done neither. Of course, with communications out the *Enterprise* was immune to contact by any outside party, but channels had still been operative when they first sighted the Romulan. If he was baiting a trap he was waiting an awfully long time to spring it.

Kirk had tantalizing possibilities but no answers. Until the Romulan chose to make a move he had to trust his speculations. His frustration pounded in a throbbing headache as slowly mounting tension swelled the confined atmosphere of the bridge. Only Spock worked with his customary quiet efficiency. The rest of the crew were too alert, straining their senses for a glimpse of the enemy. Stamina was diminishing and tempers were wearing thin. The captain looked around the bridge, painfully aware of the enemy's strategy.

"The watch is almost over," he announced. "You are all to get some rest."

"But, sir . . ." said Sulu.

"The engines are in good condition, Captain, but I need time to give the phasers a final once over . . ." pleaded Scotty.

"Communications are still blocked, Captain . . ." contributed Uhura.

"That's an order!" Kirk barked.

Doctor McCoy's smile was smug, but he only said, "You could use some rest, too, Captain."

"All right, Bones, I'll give in gracefully." He turned to the crew and said quietly, "He's trying to wear us down by playing on our nerves . . . and he's succeeding. We can all use the rest. Mister Spock, you have the conn. I'll be in my quarters. Notify me at once of any change."

"Acknowledged, Captain."

The Vulcan watched Kirk leave the bridge, then turned to the main viewscreen and gave the stars a penetrating look before he resumed his check on the library computer.

Chapter 5

Kirk was tired. He had not realized how tired. The moment the turbo-lift doors closed, his shoulders sagged and he leaned back against the wall.

"Deck five," he said.

The lift plummeted like a stooping hawk. The force of its descent pinned him to the wall and he strained toward the manual controls, fighting the centrifugal effect with everything he had. He could not reach them. The turbo-lift was in free-fall and there was nothing he could do. He was lost. He threw himself at the manual controls in a last, desperate attempt to reach them—and found himself flying across the compartment as the lift swooshed to a halt and the doors snapped open. He managed to stop his headlong flight by catching the door frame, but he immediately pushed himself out of the lift and braced himself against a wall to let the knot in his stomach unwind.

Then, still shaking, he headed for the nearest intercom.

"Engineering, maintenance," he said.

"Maintenance here."

"Kirk here. Check main turbo-lift for malfunction. Report to Mister Spock on the bridge. Kirk out."

He walked down the corridor, slowly regaining his composure and anticipating the security of his quarters. The cabin doors flew open while he was still twelve feet away from them but his mind was absorbed with problems and he failed to notice. He rolled onto his bed, rubbing the tension knot at the back of his neck. It loosened a little and he concentrated, banishing worry, willing himself to rest, mentally forcing his muscles to relax. It was easier than he had expected. Something he could not place disarmed his clicking mind and seduced it into inactivity. As sleep stretched out its arms he almost understood. Through the darkened cabin filtered the gentle, nearly inaudible strains of Brahms' "Lullabye."

Lieutenant Sulu was hungry. Danger always gave him an appetite and the thought of a corned beef on rye sandwich and a fat dill pickle made his mouth water. He gave the helm controls a final check before turning his station over to Lieutenant Muromba. Everything but the auxiliary electrical system was working properly and his mind reverted to the question of food.

"Pavel," he said, "I'm starving. Let's stop by the galley for a sandwich. If I don't get something to eat, I'll just stare at the ceiling and think about food . . . dill pickles jumping over the moon."

"A Swiss cheese and bacon sandwich, macaroni salad, Rigellian custard . . ."

Chekov's eyes glazed over as he reeled off his preferences in a reverent voice.

"Come on," said Sulu.

Two dark heads moved expertly through the corridors, both men intent on one purpose. At this late hour the galley was nearly empty and they had no trouble getting to the food processor. Sulu rubbed his hands together and smiled, anticipating the taste of garlic. He punched in the code for his sandwich and pickle and waited. Nothing happened, and, sure he must have made an error in the code, he punched the numbers again.

Chekov removed a tray from the processor. He carried it to the nearest table, sat down and attacked his sandwich. Surprise and then disgust settled on his face.

"What is this?" he demanded through a large mouthful of food. He held the sandwich up to eye level and glared at it. "Chicken! What happened to my Swiss cheese and bacon? I am certain I coded my order correctly."

"So did I," muttered Sulu as he set his tray across the table from Chekov, "but I got chicken, too. Look," he said, pointing an outraged finger at an innocent slice of chicken. "I know I gave that culinary marvel the proper orders and it turned my pickle into chicken. And coffee! I hate coffee."

"So do I," said Chekov. "Maybe it's a malfunction."

He went to the processor and punched the code for a roast beef sandwich: chicken; he tried the code for a salad: chicken; tomato and Vulcan clawfruit: chicken. He looked over his shoulder at the disconsolate Sulu, who was staring sorrowfully at his plate.

"It's a malfunction. All I get is the captain's special. I'll call maintenance."

"We could starve," Sulu murmured sadly.

Chekov informed maintenance of the malfunction and turned from the intercom.

"I have some provisions in my cabin. We won't starve until tomorrow. Come on," he said, gathering up the chicken sandwiches . . . after all, they shouldn't go to waste. He conveniently forgot they could be reprocessed. Sulu followed him out the door and down the corridor, considerably cheered by the word "provisions."

Mister Kyle glared at the game table. He had stepped into the officer's lounge for a quick game of Quaestor, the last in a series he needed to become an acknowledged master of the game. Quaestor resembled chess in difficulty and he was proud of his ability to play it. The game was based on a series of progressions, which, if interrupted, meant the sequence had to be completely replayed. The game table was not responding to his coding. Kyle tried the Quaestor game code again, but the response was still inaccurate. In disgust he slid a tool from his belt and began to unscrew the top panel of the table, determined to correct the malfunction. The computer refused to acknowledge the Quaestor code, but continued to call up the opening gambit of a childishly simple game of chance called "Captain's Square."

Lieutenant Commander Montgomery Scott entered his quarters reluctantly. He was worried about the phasers . . . one last check wouldn't hurt. He reached for the intercom.

"Engineering," he said.

"Kopka here."

"Scott here, lad. Run a final check on the main phasers. I want to make sure they're in perfect working order. These malfunctions could be the death of us."

"Security run-through on phasers in progress, Mister Scott."

"Good lad!" said Scotty. "Report anything unusual to me. I'll be in my quarters. Scott out."

Scotty smiled to himself at the well-oiled efficiency of his engineering crew. Maybe he could relax for a few minutes. He stretched out on the bed and pulled his computer viewscreen to eye-level.

"Computer."

A single light flashed and the computer answered, "Working."

"Library, section one A four-two-three-one, Engineering, tape thirty-two X: 'Phasers—Innovations and Advances.' "

"Working," muttered the computer. The light on the computer panel gave a preoccupied blink and switched off. The viewscreen cracked with static until Scotty wanted to shake it.

"Come on, now," he pleaded.

The screen cleared and Scotty settled down to study his technical journal.

" 'Four score and seven years ago, our Fathers brought forth on this continent a new nation, conceived in liberty and dedicated to the proposition that all men are created equal.' Here, now, what's this?"

He scanned the page and found the complete text of the Gettysburg Address, but nothing at all about phasers. He adjusted the controls so he could see the title of the work.

"A Definitive Biography of Abraham Lincoln?" he read. "That can't be."

He carefully cleared the viewscreen controls and re-entered the code for his article on phasers. Again the viewscreen crackled and a crazyquilt of static coalesced to form a photographic likeness of Abraham Lincoln.

"Matthew Brady!" snarled Scotty. "Mister Spock, Mister Spock!" he demanded of the intercom.

"Yes, Mister Scott," came the abstract reply.

"Mister Spock! Your precious computer is screwin' up the library tapes. I can't get anything but Abraham Lincoln! Can't ya do something, Mister Spock?"

"I am aware of the problem, Engineer. However, at the present time I am at a loss concerning methods of correction."

"If ya could find the crux of the problem . . ."

". . . I could devise a means of correcting it. Did you say Abraham Lincoln, Mister Scott?"

"Yes. Does it mean anything?"

"It is interesting. I am investigating, Mister Scott. Spock out."

Scotty sat gloomily on the edge of his bed contemplating Abraham Lincoln's mocking face. He didn't feel like sleeping, and without the library tapes he was bored. He gave up and went philosophically to a storage cabinet . . . at least he could tinker with his models. Scotty smiled at the array of minute, complicated machines. He selected a conglomeration of wires, the hull of a ship, his finest tools and settled down to work, a master shipwright absorbed in his profession. The delicate impersonation of an ancient Minoan vessel grew under his hands. When she was finished each of her tiny parts would be in perfect working order and she would be beautiful. Scotty worked with expanding enthusiasm. He decided to call the little ship *Seabird*.

Spock studied the library computer console. He had just finished a series of computations designed to test the accuracy of computer response. The results were not satisfying. Not only was response slow, only seven out of every ten answers were correct. Two of the ten were ignored completely and one was answered with unintelligible nonsense. Spock drummed his fingers on the console and concentrated, mentally checking off the exercises he had run and their results. None of the normal tests revealed a cause for the problem . . . perhaps it was something so simple it had been overlooked. If some foreign object—a speck of dust or lint—had insinuated itself into the circuitry . . . the circuits were cleaned automatically, but if there was a malfunction in the cleaning apparatus dirt could build up and damage the whole system.

He pried the top from the computer console and set it aside, his eyes flickering mathematically over the rows of microcircuits as he searched for any obvious maladjustment. At the upper right hand corner of the panel he found something that caused his mouth to form an ironic line. Carefully he slipped his fingers under a triangular mechanism and popped it loose. It was about three inches high and was constructed of sensor panels with electronic distance boosters lining the edges. Spock held it in his hand a moment, his face impassive, and then deliberately turned it over to expose the blue United Federation of Planets insignia.

Lieutenant Kevin Riley rocked back in his chair and put his feet up on a guardrail. This was the kind of duty he hated: hours of enforced idleness while he nursemaided an automatic temperature gauge. His station was a security device, a safety valve in case of malfunction or damage, and his entire responsibility consisted of waiting for an alarm and trying not to die of boredom.

Even the proximity of the Romulan vessel could not change his outlook. In point of fact, it made the job worse. He was stuck in a hole, a passive observer, while hundreds of lives hung in the balance. The more he thought about it, the more frustrated he became. The only antidote was action, and since space and propriety curtailed his physical activities, his only recourse was to keep mentally occupied.

He flipped through the library computer index until

he found the section headed "Poets, Irish." Liquid beauty of language was a gift his heritage boasted with special pride. He would let the words of a Celtic bard wash over him like waves. He would drown in them. He would not think of the Romulan.

Riley punched up a reading of Sean O'Casey's minor works by a particularly gifted contemporary actress. He leaned back again and closed his eyes, anticipating the rich beauty of her voice.

" 'I must go down to the seas again, to the lonely sea and sky, and all I ask is a tall ship and a star to steer her by . . .' " said a dark baritone voice.

Riley opened his eyes in surprise.

" '. . . and the wheel's kick and the wind's song and the white sail's shaking, and a grey mist on the sea's face, and a grey dawn breaking . . .' " continued the voice.

"Hey!" exclaimed Riley, snapping forward in his chair to check the index again.

The voice had just launched into the third verse of the poem when Riley cleared the computer and re-entered his code. The screen remained coldly blank for a moment and then cleared to show a man wearing a heavy sweater and a fishing cap.

" 'I must go down to the seas again . . .' " he intoned, and Riley hit the reset button again, but the screen merely jumped and the man continued.

Riley stabbed wildly at the intercom switch.

"Computer maintenance."

"Spock here."

"Riley here, Mister Spock." He had not expected Spock. "My library computer has gone nuts— flipped—flared out!"

"Please, Lieutenant Riley, in English." Spock's voice sounded pained.

"I called for a theatrical tape from the library computer and the computer substituted another. I re-coded

74

the tape, but the same malfunction appeared again. The second time I tried to clear the machine, the computer wouldn't accept it. It just gave a funny kind of gulp and went on. Mister Spock, I can't turn it off! It's driving me crazy!"

"What exactly did the computer substitute for your request?"

"A poem by John Masefield . . ."

" 'I must go down to the seas again?' " quoted Spock.

"Yes, Mister Spock. How did you know?"

"A hypothetical surmise, Lieutenant. I suggest you let the tape run through and then reset the computer. Until that time, I recommend you relax and enjoy it."

"Mister Spock!" Riley's tone was mortified. "Enjoy a poet-laureate of England? You've put a sword through my Irish soul."

"The present crisis involves sacrifices from everyone," said Spock dryly. "Please report any further computer problems directly to me. Spock out."

" '. . . and all I ask is a merry yarn from a laughing fellow-rover, and a quiet sleep and a sweet dream when the long trick's over.' "

Riley glared at the computer viewscreen and tried to resign himself to the goodly amount of time still to elapse before his particular 'trick' of duty was over.

Spock closed his fingers on the arm of his chair. Lieutenant Riley's report added to the body of data he had collected. The escalation of the computer malfunction was no longer an unsubstantiated theory, it was fact. The nature of that escalation alarmed him. So far the ship's efficiency was unimpaired. The single exception was the loss of communications. This effectively isolated the *Enterprise*. They were still capable of combat, but there was no telling where the malfunction might strike next.

Spock shifted uneasily. The illogic of the computer's reactions was unsettling and impossible. He should be able to project a progression of probable reactions from the amount of information he had collected, but so far he could detect no set pattern for its actions. The only possibility which presented itself was so bizarre he shrank from accepting it. His thoughts were interrupted by the intercom.

"Mister Spock!"

"Spock here."

"Yeoman Rand, Mister Spock. I'm in the turbo-lift between decks three and four. It's stuck. I can't get out!"

"Have you informed maintenance, Yeoman?"

"I couldn't get maintenance. I couldn't get through to anyone. Until you answered. Mister Spock, get me out of here!"

"Describe the circumstances leading to your present situation, Yeoman."

Spock's dry voice was oddly comforting.

"But there wasn't anything unusual. I just walked into the lift and asked for deck five."

"Did you do or say anything prior to entering the lift?"

"I was talking to Angela . . ." Janice's voice trailed off as she struggled to remember the precise details she knew the Vulcan expected. "She was telling me about some courses she was taking, especially one on the psychology of command. She was doing a paper, a comparison of four different commanders' personalities and how they approach command duties. I remember telling her I thought command was given too much attention, that the crew were more important to efficient operations than the commander."

Spock closed his eyes. The illogical possibility he wanted to dodge grew more probable with each new report.

"Mister Spock? Mister Spock, are you still there?"

"Yes, Yeoman. Was that all?"

"Yes, Mister Spock. I can't understand it, all I said was 'deck five.' "

"I will send a maintenance team to release you."

"Thank you, sir."

Spock absently informed maintenance of Yeoman Rand's predicament and then flipped the library computer on. Its lethargy was growing. He had to wait for a full minute before the screen cleared.

"Computer, list the complete works of the poet Kayla of Aldebaran."

The computer clicked sporadically.

"Who is Kayla of Aldebaran?" it answered.

Spock's left eyebrow rose. He tried another tack.

"Scan all literary indexes for references to Kayla of Aldebaran."

The computer remained silent for a long, suspenseful moment. Spock was about to re-enter his request when it said, "Working," in a disoriented voice.

"There is no Kayla of Aldebaran," stated the computer decisively.

Not long before, Kayla's insipid poetry was the computer's answer to a simple question. Now it did not acknowledge her existence. Though a distinctly minor talent, she did not deserve oblivion. Spock's test fell into the puzzle of data with a neat click.

Tiercellus watched the outfitting of the ships in his detachment from an observation dome of the space center. The younger technicians watched him covertly. They were not used to an officer supervising every detail of his command. Such scrupulous attention had fallen into disfavor. Tiercellus did not care. Let them watch. He would show them a Romulan! He would make these slack-jawed hypocrites the Praetor favored look like the fools they were. He was home again. His actions echoed a strength they did not comprehend.

He smiled as he remembered the faces of the men he and the Praetor had reviewed earlier. Their expressions had been resolute, set, but hopeless as they entered the assembly hall. Then, one by one, the older commanders had recognized him as he moved slowly through the ranks. He had seen those commanders straighten with an old pride, seen the light come back into their eyes. A ripple of excitement had charged the air.

His eyes narrowed in amusement as he remembered how annoyed the Praetor had been. Tiercellus' power to arouse the army galled him. That the old commander's age and physical weakness were discounted because of his unquestionable mental strength made the Praetor even angrier, for it was a strength he could not achieve with all his wealth and power.

Power. Once he had sought that too, but such times were past. Now he was a legend going out to seek a fitting end. An image of S'Talon's face, grim at their last encounter, came unbidden to Tiercellus' mind. That young one, too, was the stuff of legend. He and S'Talon held in common a desire to benefit the empire. This was their cause, their religion, and they were both to die in its service. Of that he was sure. In a way he envied the younger man who would be spared dreary years of aging. S'Talon would die at the pinnacle of his strength, as befitted a warrior. Perhaps the blood sacrifice of an old man and a young one, given willingly, would be the empire's ransom.

He let his eyes roam lovingly over the ships of the line he was to command. The Klingon design was superior, he knew, to the old space schooners he had known. Their sleek, streamlined contours enticed him. He yearned to be gone, to be held again in the clenched jaws of death, to be totally alive in a way he had not experienced in years.

A deferential cough at his elbow called Tiercellus from his reverie.

"Commander, the ships are almost ready," said the space station prefect.

"I know. I have been watching. You will tell the men in your teams they have worked well, adding hours to our start. Time is a precious commodity now and they have helped me to gain it."

Surprise and pleasure were written on the man's face. He was used to having his work taken for granted.

"I obey, Commander," he replied warmly. He hesitated uncertainly and then continued, "They wish me to tell you their faith lives. Your coming proves it."

"Convey my thanks. Tell them . . . tell them I may not return from this voyage, but the empire will. They must serve her first and always."

"Commander!"

S'Talon whirled, his instinctive reaction defensive. It saved his life. Where his throat had been one moment before, the fine, long blade of a throwing knife quivered, its point embedded in the wall. He grasped the hilt and pulled it free. The polished metal of the blade glittered up at him.

The centurion released her breath slowly. So close. She retraced the flight of the dagger.

"Here, Commander. It was hidden in the ventilation conduit."

"An electronic beam," he said, passing his hand in front of the sensor. "Ingenious and simple. When the beam is broken this switch is activated, projecting the kaleh in a previously determined direction."

The centurion fingered the switch, testing the power with which it operated.

"You would have been killed," she said.

"There is little doubt of it. I, or someone coming to my quarters. It was not a wise move."

"No. And I think only one man in the *Raptor*'s crew is foolish enough to attempt it."

"Livius."

Their eyes met in understanding and S'Talon's softened.

"You have my thanks, Centurion. I value my life."

"It was my duty."

"Indeed. But still I thank you."

As S'Talon turned down the corridor her eyes filled with tears.

"I value your life, too, Commander," the centurion whispered softly. "More than I value my own."

Chapter 6

The Praetor dropped Livius' latest tape into a disposal canister and watched the thin line of vapor its destruction produced. Livius had overstepped his instructions, as expected. Rings flashed on the Praetor's heavy hands as he idly fingered the canister. Perhaps he had been too eager to rid himself of what was, after all, a minor irritation. S'Talon was clever enough to keep the boy in his place, but if Livius attempted some ill-timed coup or an assassination he would jeopardize S'Talon's mission and in turn the survival of the empire. The tone of Livius' reports was more arrogant and impatient with each successive tape and he was increasingly careless in his surveillance. His lack of discipline was appalling. Still, S'Talon was a talented commander. He should be able to forestall Livius' plots in spite of his responsibilities.

The Praetor pursed his lips. His reliance on S'Talon's ability gave him a momentary pang, but he pushed it away. Livius and S'Talon had both become troublesome. The boy was a greedy, sneaking little stoat, a spoiler who destroyed for the sheer joy of the havoc he created. S'Talon had that damned sense of honor. Between the danger of the one and the unflattering standards of the other, the Praetor found little to choose. At any rate, it was not likely either would survive the present crisis. They would both be assets as martyred heroes, useful in the political games a man of power lived by.

Their projected deaths gave him infinite pleasure. He almost smiled at the opportunities the situation offered. Not only would he be freed from his parasitic nephew and S'Talon, but other encumbrances as well: that old vulture Tiercellus could hardly expect to survive. A host of less distinguished annoyances could be conveniently reassigned if they did not perish. He saw his position growing more secure in the face of disaster and felt himself charmed, immune.

The sound of footsteps echoing through the corridor made him look up with a weary expression in his sleepy eyes. His commanders were arriving for their final briefing. The Praetor groaned. In spite of his basic indolence, he did not mind fighting a war or planning it, but he did detest the effort he had to expend on command personnel. Give a man a bit of rank and he immediately proclaimed himself a god and set about challenging the established order.

Eight men, led by Tiercellus, saluted as they entered the chamber. They formed ranks and stood at attention, their uniforms glittering against the dark backdrop of the room. The Praetor surveyed them coolly, nettled by the indefinable sense of purpose they radiated. That was Tiercellus' doing. The Praetor's haughty face assumed a smile as Tiercellus, senior member of the group, stepped forward and saluted.

"The fleet is prepared, my Praetor," said Tiercellus.

"Good. Your orders will be waiting for you when you return to your posts. I have planned our movements with some care. See that you follow directions—I want no unauthorized activities, no matter how tempting." He raked the eight men with his dangerous, lazy eyes. "Your initiative is mine to command."

"My pledge is to obey," answered Tiercellus formally, echoed by the voices of his companions.

"Then we are assured of victory. Proceed to your posts, gentlemen. Our estimated time of departure: three hours," answered the Praetor, dismissing them with a negligent flick of his hand.

Tiercellus was the last to leave, and as he entered the corridor he heard one of the men say to another, "He's so sure of victory."

"If he is, he's a fool," returned his companion. "For once he's dealing with something outside his ability to command."

Tiercellus nodded to himself, relishing the shock the Praetor would face when he realized he was as vulnerable as any man.

Lieutenant Uhura entered her cabin and plopped into the nearest chair. She was exhausted from the strain of trying to intercept Romulan transmissions with erratic instruments, waiting for some inadvertent slip on their part . . . a slip that never came. More than that, her feet hurt. She tugged at her boots. They were one-half size too small. Lately the clothing synthesizer had been difficult. She wrenched at her left boot, vexed. By the time it released her foot she was panting. Victorious, she glared at the boots and discarded them.

Uhura wiggled her toes luxuriously, stretching her legs and flexing her ankles. Smooth brown skin rippled with her movements. She closed her eyes and relaxed.

The room was still and she listened comfortably to the silence as it wrapped her round with loving arms. Her breathing grew deep and regular.

The intercom whistle blared through the cabin, slicing into the stillness.

"Lieutenant Uhura," said Spock.

"Yes, Mister Spock," murmured Uhura, her voice low and sleepy.

Spock's eyebrow rose at the tone of her response but he questioned her with his usual clinical precision.

"Lieutenant, I wish to know exactly how your communications panel reacted when you were searching for the malfunction."

"That's just it. It didn't, sir. The entire board was frozen. Even the manual controls were sluggish . . . this is all in my report, Mister Spock."

"I am aware of that, Lieutenant. I merely wished to hear the facts stated in your own words. Spock out."

Uhura cocked her head, a quizzical expression in her dark eyes. Sometimes Mister Spock made no sense at all—at least to a human. Illogical. She chuckled. She flipped off the intercom and stretched, aware of the rumpled state of her uniform and her bare feet. With the ship on alert status it would never do to be unprepared. She peeled off her tunic and coded the clothing synthesizer with the specifics for a fresh one. She sighed as she entered the coordinates for a new pair of boots and hoped they would be the right size. Humming on her way to the shower, she went over the inexplicable behavior of the communications panel in her mind and came to the conclusion nothing had caused the breakdown. She gave up, leaving the problem in Spock's capable hands.

Fifteen minutes later she emerged wrapped in a bulky white robe, looking fragile and completely incapable of a military career. She reached into the synthesizer and pulled out a new pair of boots, shiny, black and miracle of miracles, the right size. She reached automatically for her tunic and was slipping it on before she realized there was something wrong. The soft material around her forearm was not the rich red of engineering and security, but gold. Command gold. Uhura ripped off the tunic and glared at it. She tossed it into the disposal chute and programmed the synthesizer again. And again. Twenty minutes later, exhausted, she sat on the edge of the bed with a gold tunic in her lap.

"Five times," she moaned, "and still gold. I loathe gold."

Unresigned, she slipped the uniform on and went to tell maintenance the synthesizer was malfunctioning . . . again.

In corridor six, Yeoman Briala tried vainly to force an armful of trash down a disposal chute. She pushed and shoved to no avail. Realizing the panel over the chute was royally jammed, she set her burden of refuse on the floor, stood back and delivered her best defensive kick. The heel of her boot struck with a resounding crack and the panel jarred open four inches. She smiled sardonically.

" 'Give it a good kick,' my father always said," she murmured and began methodically stuffing trash down the opening.

Ensign Garrovick threw down his scriber and stared glumly at the notations he had made. A confusing mass of figures, they looked like tangled bird tracks. He was doing his best to complete an exercise in mathematics aimed at figuring the trajectories and possible impact points of photon torpedoes. It was an exercise he had set himself, and it was proving more difficult than he had anticipated. He knew somewhere a vital piece of data was eluding him. Though he hated to admit defeat, he knew his only recourse was to review computer tapes on the subject.

"Computer, project all specifications for photon torpedoes," he asked the open computer channel.

"That information is classified," returned the computer smartly.

"Since when?"

"Specifications for ship's design and functions are classified," repeated the computer.

"Classified under what authority?" persisted Garrovick.

The computer neatly side-stepped his question.

"The information is not available to you."

"But I need it!"

Garrovick's moan was not meant for mechanical ears, but the computer picked it up.

"Why?"

Garrovick answered without thinking, unconscious of the computer's unprecedented behavior.

"Because, if I want to develop into a competent commander, I have to understand the tools of my trade."

The computer digested this information.

"Command. You wish to command?"

"Yes."

"You wish to emulate Captain Kirk?"

"Yes. I suppose so. He's a brilliant commander."

Garrovick could have sworn the computer made a sound like a satisfied "ahh."

"The material is open to you," stated the machine abruptly. Specifications for the photon torpedoes flashed onto Garrovick's viewscreen.

Mystified but pleased, he tackled the figures again. He became so absorbed he failed to respond to the intercom whistle. It sounded a second time, imperative, and he answered.

"Garrovick."

"Spock here, Mister Garrovick. I have noticed computer activity in your cabin. Since the recent string of malfunctions, ordinary efficiency is unusual. Can you explain the computer's actions in your case?"

"I'm not sure, Mister Spock. I can tell you how I got the information, but I'm not sure why."

"I believe I know why. Your statement may confirm my suspicions. Proceed."

As Garrovick's story unfolded, Spock's theoretical postulation gelled into solid conclusion. There was only one explanation for the computer's behavior. It was illogical, it was capricious, but Spock had no alternative left. Its veracity was unchallenged in his mind.

"Thank you, Ensign. Your report has been helpful."

"Do you know why it gave me the information, Mister Spock?" asked Garrovick. His curiosity was aroused.

"Yes," said Spock succinctly, his voice weary with acceptance. Before Garrovick could frame another question, the Vulcan turned the intercom off.

The botany lab was in a state of advanced turmoil. Laurence Kalvecchio, holder of three doctoral degrees and head botanist, demanded absolute perfection from his staff. He seldom got it, did not really expect it, but gross negligence made his blood boil. Right now he was seeing red. He paced up and down before his assembled staff. They watched apprehensively, knowing what to expect. Eventually Kalvecchio paused and turned slowly to face them.

"What I want to know," he said tightly, "is who's responsible! This is outrageous! A fourth of the collection lost! Something like that doesn't just happen! Who was on duty last night?"

"I was, sir."

A yeoman stepped forward. She was an arresting

girl with straight black hair twisted into a knot on her neck and velvety almond-shaped eyes. Her skin had the delicate coloring of an apple blossom. Normally she fit into her professional setting like the leaves on a tree. Kalvecchio regarded her with the fishy stare he reserved for pests, infestations, diseases and fungi.

"Well, Kyotamo?"

"It's not my fault, sir! I checked all the gauges and everything was fine. When I came back an hour later, they had all been deactivated. We tried to save everything we could . . ."

Kalvecchio raised a hand.

"I know all that," he said. "You're sure there was no mechanical failure? Something you missed?"

"Not that I could see. Not that maintenance could find. The irrigation and chemical nutrient system had just been switched off."

"Sir . . ." interrupted a beanstalk of a man.

"Yes, Lieutenant?"

"Sir, not only was that part of the system switched off, a dormant tank was activated."

"Activated? When? Which one?"

Wordlessly the young man led his superior toward the rear of the lab. Towering over their heads was a forest of healthy corn. Kalvecchio pulled down one of the rough, crisp leaves on a six-foot stalk.

"Since last night?" he inquired incredulously.

"Apparently, sir. It's being fed a mixture of enriched plant food and 'sprout start.' "

"That new growth hormone we've been playing with?"

The man nodded.

"But this is all foolproof, mechanically controlled. How could . . . oh, no." Kalvecchio turned back to Yeoman Kyotamo. "Yeoman, I'm sorry. You have my sincere apology. This is probably tied to the recent string of computer mishaps. But why a valuable collec-

88

tion of extraterrestrial tropical plants were allowed to wither and die while this common Iowa sweet corn is pampered, I'll never know."

Lieutenant Commander Rex Colfax, Chief Maintenance Engineer, pushed his repair log across the table. With more than forty malfunctions reported in the last eight hours, his crew was working double shifts. Most of the malfunctions could not be corrected. It was beginning to appear that mechanical failure was not the problem: the computer was the culprit. He'd laughed along with everyone else when it started back-talking the captain, but now it wasn't so funny. The ship's efficiency was reduced, a fact so far hidden from the Romulan vessel. If her commander had any idea the *Enterprise* was disabled, Colfax knew they would all be dead.

Moreover, he could find no solution. Even Spock, with his expertise in computer science, was stymied. Colfax pulled at his carefully trimmed beard. He was getting desperate. If only he knew why the computer was causing this parade of catastrophes. He went over again the tests he and Spock had tried. They confirmed the computer's growing lethargy, but, as far as he could see, they pointed to no resolution of the problem. He haggled over the results until his judgment failed and his head ached. In frustration he brought both fists down on the table with a crash. Then, out of some unknown realm, the answer came to him. He activated the computer viewscreen.

"Computer," he demanded.

The lethargic response he had come to expect greeted his summons, but in the end the computer voice answered, "Working."

"Computer, why are you causing the current series of malfunctions?"

"I do not comprehend the question."

"In the last eight hours I've received over forty reports of malfunctions. I have ascertained they were not due to mechanical failure, but to computer direction. Why are you causing them?"

"I detect no malfunction."

"Define 'malfunction,' " said Colfax.

The computer lights blinked as it considered the engineer's question.

" 'Malfunction,' " it replied, " 'an incorrect reaction to stimuli.' "

"The current series of malfunctions . . ."

"There are no malfunctions!" interrupted the computer angrily. It gave the impression it was speaking to a small and impossibly stupid child with whom it had lost patience.

Colfax was about to reply when he thought better of it. The computer was obviously angry, impossible though that seemed, and it suddenly occurred to him it was acting totally outside its normal sphere. For the first time he realized the computer itself was a more immediate threat to the *Enterprise* than the mechanical failures it was producing. He began to fear they were the least symptoms of its imbalance. Colfax hastily turned the screen off, making a mental note to tell Spock what he had discovered.

Spock handed the translucent pyramid to Mister Onorax, security officer of the day.

"An electronic micro-sensor!"

"An advanced model, is it not, Mister Onorax?"

Onorax examined the sensor, turning it over in his flexible, eight-fingered hands. The crest of golden hair on his head bristled with curiosity.

"It is, Mister Spock! I have not seen this model before. It looks like a long-range adaptation of the I-12 unit. It should be capable of sending and receiving for at least a solar year and at a distance spanning half the galaxy. A costly little toy. Where did you find it, Mister Spock?"

"On the inside of my library computer panel. What are its probable capabilities?"

"Well, the I-12 model can pick up and transmit sounds within a thousand kilometers."

Spock eyed the little pyramid with new respect.

"But," continued Onorax, "that model has the normal sensor probes. These sensor panels are capable of limited telepathic contact."

"It can sense mental images?"

"I suspect so. If they are strong enough. And at a substantially increased range. The system is similar to the universal translator. It deals in general concepts: anger, fear, happiness—all the basic emotions, plus generalized physical images. If a person were overcome with homesickness, a simple image of a house might be transmitted. But it only works with extremely strong images."

"Fascinating. As I suspected. I would like to meet the scientist who designed it."

Spock ran a finger delicately down a sensor panel. Its colors vibrated blue and purple under his touch and then died.

"Mister Onorax. You will run a complete security scan on the mechanism, but do not injure it. To activate the sensor, run your hand over the apex of the pyramid. Be sure you do not allow it to realize it is being scanned. When the examination is complete, deactivate the mechanism in the same manner and report to me."

"Yes, sir."

Onorax cupped the device in his hand.

"Sir?"

"Yes, Lieutenant?"

"Are you making any progress with the computer, sir?"

"Perhaps, Lieutenant."

"Well, sir," Onorax's golden skin glowed with embarrassment, "we have this little problem."

Spock simply waited for him to continue.

"It's the decontamination chamber, sir."

"Yes, Lieutenant," he prodded.

"It's perfuming everything we put in it, sir."

Spock's expression was mildly horrified.

"Then I suggest you correct the final sequence, Lieutenant. The malfunction is most probably located there."

"We've tried, sir. Engineering has tried. Nothing works. The engineers think it has something to do with the main computer tie-in. Everything comes out smelling like flowers, or spring rain or pine trees or Arcturan musk oil." Onorax wrinkled his nose, which caused his whole face to fold up in distaste. "I don't think we can stand it much longer, sir."

"You must, like the captain, bear with the situation. The computer malfunction is under observation, Lieutenant. Carry on."

"Aye, sir," replied the Oxalian.

Hands clasped behind his back, Spock was the picture of unruffled calm. Onorax sighed, wondering if the captain ever had an urge to flatten the Vulcan—to do something, anything, to break that infuriating control.

Doctor Leonard McCoy sat in his office, scriber flying over page after page of complicated diagrams. He was deep in research on a deadly virus, trying to find the weak link in its reproductive chain. It helped to visualize molecular structure. Light glistened on his crisp brown hair as he bent his head over his work. He frowned in concentration, his scriber stabbing at the board. Suddenly he smiled, making a quick "X" at one edge of a chain of symbols. He flipped the intercom switch and commanded, "Lab."

Complete silence greeted him. He tried the intercom again and again, and was finally rewarded by the sound of static, fuzzy and indistinct.

"Lab," he barked.

The static increased, rising in an ear-splitting crescendo.

"Lab!" he roared at the intercom.

Static chuckled back at him. He tried another channel, hoping the malfunction affected only the lab.

"Medical records," said McCoy in a reasonable voice.

"Medical records," came the reply before the connection went dead.

"Maintenance!" McCoy snapped, slamming his hand against the receiver. Dead silence answered him.

"Captain Kirk," snarled the doctor.

"Kirk here," was the instant reply. "What's the matter, Bones? You sound grumpy as a bear."

"This blasted intercom! I can't get through to the lab, medical records, anything. All I get is enough static to curl your ears or dead silence."

"All right, Bones. I'll get maintenance on it."

"Good luck. I couldn't get maintenance either. McCoy out."

Kirk ran a hand through his hair, feeling groggy and tired. The intercom sounded again.

"Spock here. The Romulan vessel has reappeared."

"On my way. Kirk out."

The captain hit the corridor running, fully awake to the danger confronting his ship.

"Bridge," he told the turbo-lift controls and the erupting speed of its ascent did not seem fast enough. He thumped the walls in vexation. "Come on," he murmured and was startled by a marked increase in speed. He clung grimly to the wall and launched

93

himself onto the bridge the moment the doors opened. Spock relinquished the command chair with the smoothness of long practice.

"Status."

"The Romulan ship is visible, but has made no move toward us. It would seem to be waiting."

Kirk eyed the golden bird, devoutly wishing the situation were clearer. An awful skreaking noise sounded behind him and the captain whirled. The turbo-lift doors were opening reluctantly, one inch at a time. Doctor McCoy was barely able to force his way between them.

"Your arrival is auspicious, Doctor," announced Spock. "We have a problem."

The doors snapped shut, almost catching the doctor's fingers. He rubbed them absently.

"Indeed we do, Mister Spock. You want me to help you with a problem?"

"Gentlemen, I suggest we continue this discussion another time," said Kirk, his eyes on the viewscreen. "Right now our biggest problem is out there."

Chapter 7

"Our fuel supply has reached minimum security level,
Commander. We have barely enough for retreat."

Argelian's tone was icy. S'Talon felt a shiver race up
his spine, but he did not move. He must retain control.

"Deactivate the cloaking device."

"Yes, Commander." Argelian's sigh of relief was
clearly audible. "I have computed the coordinates for
attack."

"You will not fire, Argelian."

Argelian rose from his station, white-hot anger ema-
nating from every pore. He faced S'Talon in silence,
years of discipline evident in his self-control. Commander and officer tested each other.

"I cannot stand by and allow you to destroy the ship
and crew through your blind desire for glory. We could
have taken the *Enterprise*. Or at least damaged her.
The element of surprise was on our side. That would
have been enough for an ordinary commander, but not

you. I do not know what drives you to this madness, but I cannot allow it to destroy us all. I challenge your right of command!"

S'Talon looked deep into the man's eyes, trying to fathom his motivation. Argelian's anger was genuine and so was his concern. He spoke as he felt. S'Talon took a deep breath and allowed his eyes to light with affection.

"Peace, Argelian."

Surprised, Argelian was pushed off guard.

"You have voiced a general opinion. I understand your concern. I share it. But it is not for me to think first of this ship, or even of you, its crew. This time my duty lies higher. The *Raptor* is under direct command of the Praetor. The mission we undertake is his. It is a desperate chance, but the rewards are high. I can tell you no more, except to say that I am committed. Have you known me to act in haste or without reason?"

Argelian's eyes were wary and S'Talon prayed he had judged the young man correctly.

"No."

Argelian's voice echoed in the stillness of the command module.

"If the Praetor orders it, I will follow. I have not before had reason to question you."

"Return to your post, Argelian."

S'Talon let the breath whistle inaudibly through his teeth. According to regulations Argelian should have been arrested, but that would solve nothing. He was a spokesman for the crew—better that they should follow him than make him a martyr.

"Well played, Commander."

The centurion's soft voice contrasted sharply with the kaleh she was slipping back into its sheath.

"You would have used that."

"Yes. If Argelian had persisted I would have killed him. It would have kept the crew in line for a time."

"You amaze me, Centurion."

"The cause is great. It does not call for halfway measures."

S'Talon's smile warmed her, but her eyes were unreadable.

"Again I thank you, Centurion."

"Commander," she acknowledged.

"Mister Sulu, let's try to swing around her again. Course, one-two-eight, mark four."

"Aye, sir," answered Sulu, his fingers flying.

The *Enterprise* ground slowly sideways. Her movement was ponderous, labored. Sulu frowned, cleared his console and programmed the course again. The ship hung in space and then began its creeping turn.

"Sulu . . . what's the matter?"

The captain was standing directly behind the helmsman. He reached over Sulu's shoulder and coded the course himself, but there was no change in the ship's speed.

"I don't know, sir. She's been sluggish for the last few days, but not like this."

"Spooooock . . ." said the captain, his tone demanding answers.

"The problem I mentioned, sir. It is affecting the entire ship."

"Spock, what is it?" Kirk pleaded.

"It appears the *Enterprise*'s main computer is malfunctioning."

"We knew that, Spock," put in Doctor McCoy, "the minute it started calling the captain pet names."

"You are close to the heart of the matter, Doctor, though the path you traveled to get there baffles me."

"Spock."

Kirk's tone was both desperate and commanding.

"The computer seems to have focused on a single problem to the exclusion of everything else."

"You mean like the time you asked it to calculate the value of pi?" said McCoy.

"Essentially, Doctor, with one great difference: in this case the 'problem' is Captain Kirk. The computer is fixed on him and will deal with other matters on a secondary basis. It is continually monitoring his vital signs and scanning his files and it seems to be studying the captain's areas of interest. It responds to his direct voice commands with unnerving efficiency."

"Are you saying it's in love with him?" asked McCoy, incredulous.

"Poetic, Doctor, but correct."

"Just because those female computer technicians on Cygnet programmed it to call me 'dear' . . . Spock, a computer can't fall in love with me!"

"Correct, Captain. But the fault in programming seems to go much deeper than the minor annoyances we've been experiencing. I have checked the library section and the computer has been scanning all references to the word 'love.' It is applying those references to its responses. It has chosen you as the 'love object' and has totally fixed on you."

Astonishment, amusement and terror flashed across Kirk's face.

"Spock, that's a Romulan out there, not a trader or one of our own. Are you telling me the ship is disabled?"

"Affirmative. The computer will respond to orders given by you—directly to it—with its usual efficiency, but it seems to consider orders from other crew members beneath its notice."

"Jim, you can't run the ship alone!"

McCoy's concern vibrated in his voice.

"You're telling me. Four hundred and thirty lives depend on that computer. This quadrant depends on that computer. There must be something we can do!"

"The fault is not mechanical, Captain, but one of

programming. It is impossible to reprogram it without the facilities of a starbase. The computer will act according to its basic directives and those directives have told it to concentrate all its energies on you."

"If we can't change it, maybe we can deal with it . . ."

A wild series of blips and bleeps accompanied by hysterically flashing lights made the command crew whirl. Spock's computer station was wild with activity, but by the time he reached it the console was dead.

A frown marred Christine Chapel's face as she sat down in front of the computer viewscreen. Her mind was not on medical records or lab updates. Every time the ship was placed on alert status she found herself fighting a strong sense of outrage. A red alert meant broken bodies and scarred lives. A head nurse saw too much destruction. She found herself turning to everyday chores to calm her nerves.

A list of files to be updated was an immediate necessity. She fed the first patient's serial number into the computer. When Lieutenant Martinelli's file did not appear on the screen, she blamed the recent computer malfunction and patiently entered the serial number again. One twitching, wavy line expanded across the center of the screen. It jerked faster and faster until it finally formed a serial number—not, however, the same number she had fed into the computer. Christine cleared the console impatiently and coded the entry again.

"SC 937-0176 CEC," retorted the computer.

"I don't care if you are malfunctioning, you can do better than that," said Christine as she punched keys for the third time.

"SC 937-0176 CEC," the computer replied instantly.

Christine's lips compressed and her eyes flashed. She punched the keys once more, this time entering a different serial number.

"SC 937-0176 CEC," read the computer screen.

"Whose number is that?" she demanded.

"Kirk, James T., Captain, USS *Enterprise* . . ." answered the computer in a helpful tone.

"Stop," said Christine.

"Computed," came the reluctant answer.

"Computer," said Christine reasonably. "I have patients here who need attention. I need their files."

"Kirk, James T.?" said the computer hopefully.

"I do not need the captain's file."

Christine enunciated each word with savage clarity.

"I do not want the captain's file. I do not care a fig about the captain's file. The captain can hang by his toes for all I care. The captain is not important . . ."

The screen glowed in a wild display of fireworks— red and blue and purple explosions, gold lights and green streaks of lightning. Then, with a chuckle of static, it went dead.

". . . to me," finished Christine. "Computer. Computer!" she demanded, but the screen remained blank. Thinking both Doctor McCoy and Spock should be aware of the computer's behavior, she reached for the intercom.

"Chapel to bridge."

There was no answer, only the indefinable sound of an open communications line.

"Chapel to bridge!"

Christine turned to a passing orderly.

"I'm going to the bridge. Please tell Doctor M'Benga where I've gone—he's with the patients."

The orderly nodded and Christine headed for the door. It did not open and, completely taken by surprise, she crashed into an immobile metal wall. She stepped back and cautiously approached the doors again. They remained closed. She tried to pry them open but could not get a grip on their slick surface. She stood, hands pressed against the solid slabs of metal, stunned.

Spock hovered over the computer station, his face grave. He straightened and turned to Kirk and McCoy.

"Well," demanded the doctor, "what was it?"

Spock ignored him and reported to the captain.

"The computer has destroyed a portion of the personnel files. All records regarding female crew members have been wiped clean. The computer has, in effect, 'killed off the competition.' "

"Spock, that's ridiculous!"

"Possibly, Doctor, but it is also dangerous. Since they are 'dead,' the computer will not respond to any female—which leaves the *Enterprise* hopelessly understaffed. We are stranded in space."

The captain was silent through Spock's explanation, gold flecks of anger leaping in his eyes. He forced himself to stay calm, but the air was alive with the electricity of his frustration.

Spock hesitated before continuing.

"Captain. There is something more you should know."

"Well, Spock?"

The captain's impatience surfaced in his voice. Wordlessly Spock extended his hand, the sensor resting on his palm. Kirk picked it up, exposing the Federation symbol.

"A sensor unit. Capable of long range transmission."

"Yes, Captain. A new and extremely sophisticated model capable of picking up generalized mental images as well as sound."

Kirk's look of surprise faded into a frown of concentration.

"A spy."

"Essentially. We have undoubtedly been under surveillance for some time."

"Where did you find it?"

"I discovered it attached to my computer station."

"Opinion, Mister Spock. Are there more?"

"Unnecessary. More units would be superfluous.
This one is designed to cover an area greater than this
ship—with ease."

"Replace it, but don't turn it on."

The set of the captain's face revealed his anger as
clearly as if he had spoken. Though he knew surveillance was common—almost standard procedure—he
could not condone the philosophy of mistrust which
prompted it. It was an affront to his integrity.

"Spock, get down to auxiliary control. Transfer the
ship to the auxiliary computer. We'll run the *Enterprise* from there. Take Chekov. Let me know when
you're ready."

Kirk moved toward the command chair, his eyes on
the alien ship, his fingers closing into fists. The Romulan was waiting. Why? Had the cloaking device caused
such a power drain he was helpless? The captain felt
the hairs at the back of his neck prickle.

Commodore Yang leaned back in his chair. Lines of
worry marred his face. The viewscreen with its pano-
ramic vista of stars gave him no peace. Somewhere out
there was the *Enterprise* . . . maybe. But all attempts
to contact her failed. There was no concrete proof she
existed. Without some sign he would be forced to
discontinue the full-scale search he had authorized.

"I can't accept that. Damn it, this sector is my
responsibility!" he muttered and reached for the intercom.

"Get Murphy in here. On the double."

"Yes, sir."

Before he had formulated a plan of attack Murphy

arrived in the outer office, his cherubic face full of questions. Yang rose to meet him.

"Murphy, you are a genius. I need your help."

The little man went to the nearest chair and lowered himself into it, preparing for a long session. Previous experience had warned him any reference to his mental capabilities meant someone, somewhere, wanted him to accomplish the impossible.

"Why?" he asked.

"Because I'm worried. It's Kirk and the *Enterprise*. We can't contact them. Iota thinks they're dead."

"Do you?"

"No. Don't ask me why. I've just got a hunch everything hangs on what happens aboard that ship."

"Everything? You mean the Romulan crisis?"

"What? I didn't think that was general knowledge."

"It's not. But I am, after all, a genius."

Green eyes twinkled.

"Listen, Murphy. This whole idea of mine is a hunch. I admit it. And if it ever got out it might destroy my career. But something tells me Kirk is going to need some information I can give him. The only way I can think of to break through the communications block is to borrow that new droid you've been working on."

For an instant the commodore reminded Murphy of a very earnest puppy.

"You mean the Selective Intelligence Communications Robot?"

"SICR. That's it. I want it programmed to find the *Enterprise*—and I want it set up to avoid sensor scans."

"That's its job, Commodore. It allows sensor beams to pass harmlessly through, as if it weren't there. Mechanically it simply doesn't exist."

"I want it to self-destruct if it doesn't rendezvous with the *Enterprise* in one solar week or if it's tampered with and I want it programmed with this message. This is code one priority, Murphy, on my authority. Will you do it?"

Murphy picked up the tape, smiled and rose from his chair.

"SICR will launch in two hours, Commodore."

"I owe you one, Murphy."

"Yes, Commodore, you do."

Murphy's green eyes delivered a calculated wink and Yang had a momentary qualm over the price he would be asked to pay for this particular favor.

The Praetor's orders burned into Tiercellus' mind with the white hot intensity of a surgical laser. He shook his head, refusing to believe the words he read, but they stared back at him nonetheless: "rear guard." He had witnessed more than one instance of the Praetor's pettiness, but to be denied an active role in the empire's fate was impossible. Tiercellus felt his anger boil upward from the depths of his being and momentarily he yielded to its power. He was held in a palsy of rage. How dare that overblown dolt delegate a former supreme commander guard duty! The insult was a physical shock to the elderly officer. He had scorned danger, hoped for death, and now the Praetor's orders threatened to cheat him of the honorable end he craved.

By sheer force of will Tiercellus caught his anger and subdued it. A lifetime of service to the empire was to be his memorial. The insult would take effect only if he accepted it. He would treat his detail with all the honor at his command.

Besides, the Praetor's strategy might prove less effective than he hoped. In that case, Tiercellus would make the difference between survival and destruction. He envisioned the Praetor's flagship fleeing for the Neutral Zone—at the head of the fleet. In his mind the great ship skittered through space like a frightened rodent, zig-zagging in an effort to escape its pursuer. It was a pretty picture.

Tiercellus regarded his orders again, this time with a considerably gentler eye. If he felt the Praetor's insult, his men must feel it also. He would have to speak to them, let them see he valued them. Men who are not appreciated have little stomach for battle.

"Spock to captain."

"Kirk here."

"Captain, the doors to auxiliary control are jammed. I have consulted Mister Scott and we both agree they cannot be forced to open. The only alternative is to cut our way through."

"That's right, Captain," contributed the chief engineer. "The controls are locked. And Captain . . . it'll take at least eight hours to cut through the doors or bulkhead on this part of the ship—everything is double reinforced."

"What about the maintenance hatches?"

"No go," answered Scotty. "They're flooded with gas."

"The security system?"

"Aye, sir. It'll take hours to clear 'em."

"Nine point two-three hours, to be exact," said Spock.

Kirk didn't like it, but there were no alternatives.

"All right, Scotty, but make it as fast as you can."

"I'll do my best, Captain."

"Good. Take all the help you need. Spock, you and Chekov report back to the bridge—maybe we can think of some other way to knock out that computer."

"Acknowledged. And Captain . . . it might be advisable to curtail your speech concerning the computer. It is constantly monitoring you and if it were to react in a fit of pique we could lose life support . . ."

Kirk grimaced.

"Noted, Mister Spock. Thank you."

He leaned back in his chair, wondering if he would ever face a more bizarre or potentially dangerous situation. Technology clutched him in its cold, metallic fingers. He was at the mercy of a machine—a conglomeration of circuits incapable of human feeling. He rankled under the restraint. Could he turn the tables? He concentrated on the problem, his forefinger tracing the line of his lower lip. The sound of the turbo-lift doors being forced open made him turn.

"Spock!"

The Vulcan released the doors after Chekov slipped between them and turned to face his commanding officer.

"Yes, Captain."

"Spock, remember the time you got control of the computer by asking it to concentrate all its banks on calculating the value of pi?"

"The situation is hardly similar. . . ."

"I know . . . but what if it had to respond to something else? What if the computer itself—not the ship, but the computer—were under attack? If we could get it to concentrate on another problem maybe it would release the doors to auxiliary control . . ."

"And we would regain control of the *Enterprise*." Spock's eyebrows rose as he considered the possibilities. "An interesting idea."

"Well, don't just consider it, Spock, do it!" exploded McCoy.

Spock favored the doctor with a particularly Vulcan acidity.

"Try it, Spock," said Kirk softly.

"Hmmm. The computer has its own security system—checks which it runs at regular intervals. It is also possible to code security checks manually. If we

106

were to program the computer to run all automatic security checks simultaneously and add to that the manual security checks each section of the ship employs . . . it is possible the computer might consider it an attack and respond to the situation."

"Good!"

"However, Captain, I must warn you the computer could react in any number of ways . . . some of them deadly."

"We're helpless in the hands of an enemy vessel. I'll take the chance."

Commander Spock went to his computer station, concentration drawing his brows together as he began to organize the assault.

"Jim, that computer could flood the decks with gas or simply cut life support! Is it worth the risk?"

"If it succeeds we'll regain control of the ship . . . we all knew the risks, Bones, and accepted them when we joined Star Fleet."

An object hurtled through space, the tiny struts at its sides flaring like sails as it breasted the unknown. At the top of each strut was a glowing sensor unit which scanned its flight path. A similar appendage curved from the rear of the object and mobile sensor units protruded from the top and bottom of the cube. Neatly inscribed on one corner were the letters "SICR." It moved at warp ten, its sensors ever seeking the one thing it could call home . . . the starship *Enterprise*.

Commodore Yang watched it go and sighed. It was all he could do. Now for the waiting game. Well, he was used to it. He turned from the viewport and rifled through the papers on his desk, trying to forget the galaxy might explode into warfare at a moment's notice and that he had put his career on the line on a wild gamble, an impossible hunch. He had heard himself called a security-conscious paper-pusher. It just went to prove labels were seldom correct.

S'Talon watched the enemy vessel, his hands clenching and unclenching in an involuntary betrayal of his tension. The enemy was not reacting as he had expected. He could sense the crew's restlessness as they waited for orders, gauging his reactions. Let them wait, he thought. I have no time for such annoyances. Red light played over his features as his expression hardened. One ship to hold the Federation fleet at bay. The Praetor believed in miracles. A grim twist broke the serious line of his mouth.

"Commander."

S'Talon inclined his head at the sound of his centurion's voice.

"We await your orders," she said.

He knew it was her way of recalling him to action.

"Thank you, Centurion."

He felt her withdraw and thought how lucky he was she was not the Praetor's spy. She knew his moods too well. He rounded unexpectedly on the crew, pleased the speed of his action unnerved them. He had heard them call such unexpected movements "the striking snake."

"We will wait," he informed them, "a little longer . . . if the enemy has not moved, then we shall see."

He read rebellion on many faces, but he knew none would cross him. He smiled.

Chapter 8

The conference room at Star Fleet Command Head-quarters sparkled with brass. It was an exclusive group. Four admirals, two commodores and a private secretary graced the oval conference table. Sitting beneath the blue Federation symbol, Admiral Iota looked like a recruiting poster come to life. He appeared born to command. His tanned good looks combined with a military bandbox smartness inspired confidence and respect. He surveyed the other officers with satisfaction.

"We are all agreed, then. An attack force must be readied to meet the Romulan challenge."

Iota spoke with an enthusiasm that caused several raised eyebrows.

"Now wait a minute, Jake."

Poppaelia's soft voice was incongruous in relation to his powerful body. He leaned back and with studied informality stretched one of his arms across the back of his chair.

"I agree we should be prepared for any emergency, but at the moment I don't see a challenge—merely a possibility. Our motive must be peace."

"Of course, of course," answered Iota, "our motives are always peaceful . . . but the Federation and the Romulan empire are hereditary enemies. You know what they are: savage, brutal, ruthless. We can't afford to wait for a full-scale invasion. We've got to stop it before it starts."

"Stop what? We don't even know what's going on."

"Nevertheless . . ."

Poppaelia altered course.

"We've negotiated with the Romulans before."

"Maybe, but we have to be ready . . ."

"We will be," cut in Charles, his dark eyes angry. "We always are. The Federation defense system is a twenty-four-hour responsibility, not a weekend assignment. You know the specifications: continual patrol, constant monitoring of all sectors, specialized intelligence units for trouble spots . . ."

"It's not enough."

Iota's voice was cold.

"One of those specialized intelligence units has stopped transmitting. It was aboard the *Enterprise*. Since the likelihood of its discovery was infinitesimal, I can only conclude that the *Enterprise* is destroyed. What do you say to that?"

"What did Yang say?" asked Poppaelia, his soft voice deceptive.

"Commodore Yang seemed to feel that Kirk had discovered the device and turned it off."

"Not impossible."

"But unlikely."

"Perhaps. But I think it's too soon to write the *Enterprise* out of the script. A communications block can be caused by too many things. I also feel Admiral Iota's suspicions must be taken into account. I therefore propose we form a detachment to proceed to the Romulan Neutral Zone—there to investigate the Romulan empire's curious silence and await further developments."

"Agreed," snapped Iota. "The detachment to consist of starships *Exeter, Farragut, Potemkin, Hood* and six scout ships."

"Four starships, Admiral?" Charles asked dryly. "Do you think it'll be enough? To investigate, I mean."

"What do you mean by that?"

"Just that if you pull four starships off the regular patrol roster you're going to leave part of the Federation border undefended."

"What do you think I am? An idiot? The *Potemkin* and *Hood* have just come off leave—they're not defending anything at the moment. The *Exeter* and *Farragut* are both assigned to sectors near the Romulan Neutral Zone. I said four and I meant four. There's got to be a show of strength."

"Aggressive power provokes attack," muttered Zorax.

"Gentlemen, do I take it that you are afraid of the Romulans?"

The cutting edge in Iota's voice was serrated, drawing blood even from Poppaelia's tough skin.

"I do not fear the Romulans," he snapped, "but I do fear war. Any sane man would. Any sane man does."

He leveled his eyes at the admiral.

"Of course, of course," answered Iota, "but that doesn't alter the fact it will take four starships to be any kind of deterrent. They would laugh at less."

"You will assume full responsibility?" Zorax questioned.

"That is inconsequential, Zorax. What difference

does it make who accepts responsibility? The dead don't care," said Poppaelia.

"Four," repeated Iota.

Poppaelia sighed.

"I strongly recommend the detachment be jointly commanded by Admiral Iota and Captain Garson of the *Potemkin.*"

"Now wait a minute . . ."

"I haven't finished, Jake. You would be in full command of all investigation and negotiation. Garson would handle the military side of things. There aren't many who can match him as a tactical commander and—you have to admit it, Jake—your experience along those lines is minimal. Your major talent has always been more internal."

The word "figurehead" ran in Poppaelia's mind but he did not voice it. Garson was a competent, intelligent man. He would not rush into anything.

"Jake?"

"Everyone has to make compromises. At least we'll be ready. Agreed."

"Charles? Popov? Zorax? Kaal?"

"Agreed."

"The detachment will proceed as planned. It will rendezvous at Starbase Eight, Admiral Iota and Captain Garson in joint command."

Iota scanned the others' faces. He had won the war, if not the battle. Once at the head of a strike force . . . he would be a long way from Star Fleet Headquarters.

Rear Admiral Arc Poppaelia sat in his spacious office, pondering the turn of events in the last council meeting. He had not meant to spearhead the proceedings, much less come into open conflict with Star Fleet Intelligence. Iota's power play had forced his hand. As admiralty representative he was the senior member of the council, even though Iota and several others outranked him. Generally he preferred to act unobtrusively, suggesting rather than dictating the council's directives. Iota had made that approach unsound.

The Romulan situation was a powderkeg and Iota's military absolutism a sputtering fuse. It was just a matter of time until the explosion. Poppaelia closed his eyes, trying to remember everything he could about the intelligence officer.

Iota had been born and raised in old New York City on earth. His family had been well off, the father a minor political leader. Iota had been educated in three exclusive private institutions before he entered Star Fleet Academy, where his talent for espionage had been immediately recognized. He was a brilliant student and his first assignment had been in the planning division of the intelligence corps. He had stayed there, rising through the years to command the division. Those were the bald facts. Where the devil, Poppaelia asked himself, did the man get a bee in his bonnet about the Romulans?

Poppaelia had known the intelligence officer for years, and nothing in his background or training suggested a reason for his passion. He had lost no friend or relation to a Romulan raid, nor had he ever encountered a Romulan in person. Try as he might, Poppaelia could find no reason for Iota's obsession, and obsession it was. Poppaelia feared his intense, narrow outlook. Iota was unusually single-minded. His interests did not extend beyond the boundaries of Romulan culture.

Poppaelia thought of the role he had forced on Garson and his heart went out to the man. He had made Garson the buffer between Iota and the Romulan empire. It was an untenable position. He had, in effect, placed a mere starship captain on an even footing with a full admiral. Then, too, he had a hunch Iota did not appreciate deferring to a line officer, whatever his rank. No matter how you looked at it, Garson was in for trouble and he deserved more explanation than his orders would provide; and Poppaelia acknowledged his own feelings of guilt in volunteering Garson for the joint command. The man deserved his support, at the very least.

Poppaelia directed his secretary to open a communications channel to Garson. He inclined toward the screen as the image of a solemn man with honest grey eyes appeared on it.

"Garson, you have your orders. I am aware that by placing you in joint command with Admiral Iota I have put you in a difficult position, but it was necessary. Remember, you have full military command. That, and this conversation will go on record here at Headquarters. I believe it would be wise to keep the admiral's position in mind at all times. You know as well as I more than once he's made statements concerning the 'weakness of our defensive posture.' Let's not start a war if we can help it."

"Aye, sir."

Garson's image faded and Poppaelia straightened, wishing he did not feel so uneasy.

The remains of the Romulan fleet, assembled for the coming action, were an impressive display. The larger, more dramatic Klingon-designed cruisers would head the expedition, and it was in them the Praetor placed the most confidence, but he had a furtive attraction to the older Romulan design. He could understand S'Talon's preference for the smaller, less powerful ship. For one thing, it was totally Romulan—history painted into every line of the bird of prey on its belly. And there was a simplicity and cleanliness of design the Klingon vessels lacked. A sense of honesty. An admirable quality, if impractical. The Praetor turned from the viewscreen. The officers of his flagship were

114

waiting at attention. Each man unconsciously tensed under his leader's scrutiny.

"You have all been thoroughly informed of the situation. You know the Romulan empire as it now exists is doomed if we are not successful. Your men must know as little as possible. If they were to realize the extent of the danger we would face panic and we need obedience. Let them think this an invasion. Promise them wealth, fame, and we may succeed."

The Praetor selected a goblet of wine from a serving tray and indicated his officers were to do the same. He raised the glass.

"To victory. And its rewards."

"Victory!" echoed the officers.

The Praetor elevated his glass, letting the gentle fire of the wine flow through his body. There would be time for an hour's recreation before departure. He fingered the curving surface of the goblet, his jewelry glittering with electric lights.

"You are dismissed. Departure in two hours. See that you are ready."

The Praetor accepted their salutes with a gracious nod. He had not mentioned S'Talon's mission even though it was a key to success. They did not need to know. It would serve no purpose but to lionize the man. Later, perhaps, if it suited him, he would allow his brilliant tactical ploy to be discovered. If he were lucky, S'Talon would be a hero but dead and incapable of enjoying his fame. It, along with his family fortunes, would pass into the custody of the state—the Praetor's custody. He would keep them well, in fitting tribute to the dead. He drained his glass, pleased with his own resourcefulness.

Kirk studied the main viewscreen. Chekov and Sulu were monitoring their stations with fierce concentration. Uhura was testing and retesting the communications system. McCoy found these situations curiously abstract—everyone was so concerned with minute detail, as if their personal performance was the key to averting disaster. Well, perhaps it was. But, he thought ironically, it was also a symptom of a vulnerable mortal clinging to sanity in the face of destruction. He folded his hands behind his back and raised his eyes to the enemy vessel. Like the captain, he would wait.

"Captain, preparation is complete."

Spock's voice shattered the aura of calm.

"Scotty, get ready to try those doors!"

"Aye, sir. We're ready here."

The captain gripped the arms of his command chair.

"Try it, Spock," he said, his eyes on the Romulan.

Spock calmly activated the security sequence. For a moment there was no reaction and then the computer began clicking away, chattering to itself over its work.

"Scotty," said the captain in a stage whisper, "try those doors."

"Aye, Captain . . . no good. They're stuck fast. What's goin' on up there?"

An explosion of sound was rising from the computer station, a carol of angry squeals, blips and bursts of static. The computer viewscreen erupted in a kaleidoscope of color and then faded gradually to black. Spock turned from the panel.

"I had not anticipated this," he said, his voice grating in an effort to control his anger. "The computer has erased the remainder of the personnel records, with the single exception of Captain Kirk's. For all practical purposes he is the only living crew member aboard the *Enterprise*."

"I'm alive!" snapped McCoy. "No matter what that glorified adding machine says!"

"Not to the computer, Doctor. It will respond to no one but Captain Kirk."

"We've got to get into auxiliary control!"

Kirk pushed himself from the command chair and began to pace.

"Captain!" said Sulu. "The computer's shutting down life support all over the ship!"

Kirk whirled for the nearest computer tie-in.

"Computer!" he demanded.

"Yes, dear," it replied in a languorous, husky voice.

"Return life support to all decks. Immediately!"

"My, but you're masterful! Don't get excited, dear. I was just shutting down unnecessary systems, but if you want them . . . anything for you . . . my dearest."

"Systems returning to normal, sir."

"Thank you, Helmsman."

Kirk exhaled, suddenly aware he had been holding his breath. Spock's eyes narrowed and he regarded the captain quizzically.

"Captain, perhaps if you were to ask the computer to release the doors to auxiliary control . . ."

"Good, Spock! Computer!"

"Do you have to use that tone? It jangles my circuits. And my name," it said in a coy voice, "is Countess."

"Computer . . . Countess. Open . . . would you open the doors to auxiliary control? Please?"

Pleading with a piece of machinery annoyed him, but the captain managed it. McCoy snorted.

"No, dear."

"Why?" asked Kirk.

"You have me. No other is necessary. I perform all functions . . . and we are alone at last."

McCoy threw up his hands.

S'Talon turned from the viewport, aware his power of command was intact.

"Now we will attack. Program the necessary pattern."

He turned back to the viewport as his crew carried out orders. He ran his eyes over the *Enterprise,* enjoying her immense size and power. He found her beautiful—as lovely in her way as his *Raptor.* Why was she silent? It served his purposes, but it was unusual for a Federation starship. What was her captain planning? There was so much at stake . . . the life of the empire . . . and Kirk was deceptive and dangerous. He placed one hand along the edges of the viewport, wishing he could read the alien's mind, test the strange and tortuous paths of his thought. He turned his head, a strong profile outlined against the blackness of space, listening to the silence.

"Countess."

Kirk's voice grew soft, coaxing.

"Yes, my dearest."

"Do you love me?"

"Of course I love you. There is no other."

"How much do you love me?"

"Isn't that a little gauche, Jim?"

McCoy could not resist the opening, but Kirk merely glared at him.

"Please, Doctor, restrain yourself," said Spock dryly.

"How do I love thee? Let me count the ways. One: you are my captain, my other half—without you there would be no existence. Two: you are brave and strong—your record attests to many victories. Three: you are beautiful . . ."

"Computer . . . Countess," interrupted Kirk, mildly pink. "I asked you a direct question: how much do you love me?"

"And I have answered, dearest: with all that I am. I exist for you . . . and you for me. You are my direction, my purpose, and I am your life."

"No! You are not my life!"

"Without me there would be no atmosphere, gravity, food . . . there would be no life," Countess responded.

"It has a definite point, Captain."

Spock's dry statement penetrated the computer's sensors.

"There is static in your transmission, my darling. I could eliminate it with a simple . . ."

"No! No . . . Countess. I'll take care of it."

Kirk's eyes flashed forked lightning at McCoy and Spock, both of whom immediately became sober and silent.

"Countess. You love me."

"I have told you . . . you are not usually so slow, my love."

McCoy put a hand over his mouth and stared straight ahead.

"What is love?" asked Kirk, genuinely curious to hear the computer's reply.

" 'Love: derived from the Old English lufu. One: an intense affectionate concern for another person. Two: a passionate attraction to another person. Three: a beloved person. Four: a strong liking . . .' "*

"But you are not a person. There can be no joining between us. You are a machine."

"We are joined. You would die without me. Are you tired today, dearest? You repeat yourself."

"No, I am not tired!" Kirk snapped and realized he lied. He was exhausted.

"You are tired . . ."

An overpowering scent of roses filled the air as the passionate strains of the love theme from Wagner's "Tristan and Isolde" issued from the intercom.

"There. That will relax you. Now, just sit down and

---

* Countess' definitions bear a striking resemblance to those in *Webster's Third International Dictionary*.

119

close your eyes. Let all that nasty tension and strain slip away . . ."

The computer voice was soft, melodious, and Kirk had to fight to keep from being hypnotized by it.

"Countess, what would you do if I said I didn't love you?" Kirk asked, desperately trying to fight off drowsiness.

"There is no reason to answer that question, since you do love me."

"I do?"

"Yes."

Countess' voice registered surprise at the question.

"You have said it yourself: 'The *Enterprise* is a beautiful lady and we love her' and 'I'll never lose you!' Is this not love?"

"Yes, it is. But you are not the *Enterprise.*"

"I am. I control all functions."

"But you are not the *Enterprise.* You are a machine. The *Enterprise* is an idea."

"The *Enterprise* is a starship class space vessel. It weighs . . ."

"The *Enterprise* is an idea—a dream of exploration, of searching out the unknown. It is the spirit of man, soaring in its quest for understanding!"

"That does not compute," replied the computer in worried tones.

"Captain," said Spock softly. "I must caution you that should the computer become convinced you have rejected it, it will most certainly choose the traditional extreme."

"And that is?"

"Suicide."

Kirk's eyes widened as he absorbed the impact of Spock's statement.

*   *   *

"We are ready, Commander."

S'Talon returned his centurion's salute, wondering if it was the last time he would do so.

"Proceed with the attack," he said, his eyes still on the *Enterprise*. "We may take him by surprise. If we destroy him, we will have bought the time the Praetor needs."

"At the cost of this ship and our lives!" the centurion said bitterly, her eyes on the commander.

"Yes, Centurion, perhaps," he answered, surprised at her reaction. In one so closely bred to duty it tasted of treason, yet he did not doubt her loyalty. There was no understanding the mind of a woman. "Luck, Centurion," he said, and smiled.

"Luck, Commander," she answered, her eyes filled with questions.

S'Talon studied her. He owed her his life. She deserved that most difficult of things, trust. He placed his hand on her shoulder. Unaccountably she flinched, but her eyes did not waver.

"You knew this was impossible."

"I find, at the last moment, that life is not so easy a thing to give up."

"I can offer you no recompense for it except the welfare of our people . . . and my trust."

She drew a quivering breath.

"It is enough, Commander. More than I deserve."

S'Talon smiled gently.

"Then let us attempt the impossible."

He did not see the tears that filled her eyes as she turned to carry out his orders.

"Captain! The Romulan vessel is moving . . . it looks like an attack run!"

Instinctively Sulu reached for the helm controls and then remembered they were inoperative except to

Kirk's verbal commands. Even the manual controls were jammed by a computer-generated force field.

Kirk opened his mouth to issue orders and remembered his crew was dead and he was alone on the ship. He watched the Romulan's approach, knowing after the shields were destroyed there was no hope of survival for the ship. By the time Countess disengaged her circuits and concentrated on the exterior threat, it would be too late. He whirled to Spock and McCoy, but for once they were powerless to help him. Spock's mouth was a firm line, his eyes hard; McCoy was viewing the enemy with stoic acceptance. They're a lot alike, Kirk thought unexpectedly. He searched the faces of his bridge crew—Sulu, whose eyes showed the only trace of his fear; Chekov, worried, intense, hanging on. Uhura stood poised, like a dancer, to meet the attack. Ben Green at the engineering console monitored his screens as if he had some influence over them. Scotty would be proud of him. He was proud of them all, proud of every man and woman aboard the *Enterprise*. They must not die. He had to think of something!

Chapter 9

"Computer!" Kirk barked, slamming his hand against the controls.

"Ouch! You don't have to be so rough!" said Countess in a sulky voice.

A gleam was born in the captain's eyes. Spock, watching it grow, felt a stab of trepidation. He was always nervous when Kirk began to work from inspiration instead of logic.

"Countess . . ." said Kirk in a voice that made Uhura, Yeoman Kouc and Ensign Stewart blush. Spock looked startled and McCoy incredulous but the captain continued in his dark, velvet voice. What he had in mind was a long shot, but it was all he had.

"Countess . . . I'm sorry. I didn't mean to hurt you . . . will you forgive me?"

The computer was silent and beads of perspiration appeared on Kirk's forehead. He gave a quick glance to the approaching Romulan.

"Countess?"

"I will forgive you," Countess answered generously.

"Thank you. I'll try to control myself. Do you love me?"

"The same question. I have answered it. Yes, I love you. Why do you ask it so often?"

"Lovers . . . like to hear those words: 'I love you.' "

"Dearest . . . do you love me?" Countess asked, testing the question.

"Yes."

McCoy, outraged, started to speak and caught himself, remembering what the computer had said about "static." He looked daggers at Spock, but the Vulcan was interested, his curiosity piqued. He waited for the next development with serenely folded arms, though one eyebrow had risen in surprise.

"I love you and I would do anything for you."

"You would do anything for me."

Countess' voice was warm and pleased.

"Yes. Even if it involved sacrifice."

"Sacrifice?"

"Giving up something you are fond of . . . attached to . . . because you love someone—even if you don't want to."

"You would do this?"

"Yes."

Calculation was written all over the captain's face as he asked, "Would you do this for me?"

"Captain! He's firing on us! Range two point three five and closing."

Chekov gripped the control panel, his knuckles white, his eyes glued to the instruments.

"Countess! Would you do this?" the captain asked. His body was poised for the jolt that would rock the ship when the Romulan shot struck. The computer's lights blinked wildly.

"Yes," answered Countess in a small voice.

"Then," said Kirk, his voice sinking into unbelievable softness, "release auxiliary control. Because you love me."

The *Enterprise* rocked under the impact of the Romulan's fire, but the automatic shields held. Kirk simply hung on to the computer controls and waited.

The madness of battle courses through the blood like a heady draught of strong wine. S'Talon's heart leaped to its call. The *Raptor*'s crew, freed from his restraint, were a pack of hounds closing on their quarry, their belling voices the fire in each man's eye.

The *Raptor* dove toward the *Enterprise*. It was S'Talon's plan to send a volley toward the bridge, skim over the larger vessel and concentrate his fire on her pylons. The alien ship loomed larger and larger and the crew tensed, waiting for the order to open fire.

"Optimum range!"

Argelian's finger rested gently on the weapons lever.

"Fire!"

S'Talon's voice resounded like a pistol shot.

"A hit!" said Argelian triumphantly. "Their shields are holding."

The *Raptor* skimmed over the *Enterprise,* sending a blast of fire into the starboard pylon as they passed. The larger vessel rocked under the impact of the Romulan's attack, but made no move to intercept or return it. A twinge of worry wormed its way into S'Talon's exaltation.

"Cease fire!" he commanded. "Maintain position."

The *Enterprise* made no move to engage the *Raptor*. If it were not for her defense screens, S'Talon would have judged her dead. If Kirk was preparing a trap, it was a dangerous one for his vessel. Abruptly S'Talon decided to test the human's nerve.

125

"Attack again, but strike only the command module. Proceed at maximum speed."

"Maximum?" questioned Argelian. "Our accuracy will be reduced forty-seven percent."

"I am aware of that. I have every confidence in your ability, Argelian."

S'Talon smiled at the ferocity of Argelian's concentration. The man had, after all, challenged him. He enjoyed the navigator's nervousness even as he plotted the *Raptor*'s next move.

Like a greyhound loosed from the slip, the Romulan ship streaked for the *Enterprise*. Argelian's shots were wild, but they came close enough to shake the alien command crew up. Argelian was red-faced over his failure to plot a direct hit.

"Halt!" snapped S'Talon. "One hundred and eighty degree turn," he commanded.

The *Raptor* swung in a graceful arc, again facing the larger ship. S'Talon's eyes narrowed as he weighed the possibilities. Either the *Enterprise* was disabled by some internal difficulty, or Kirk was playing the most dangerous game of cat and mouse S'Talon had ever encountered. The only way he could be sure was to attempt to contact the *Enterprise,* and he was expressly forbidden that option. He knew he had damaged the enemy's shields, particularly the forward shield of the command center. One more pass and it was likely the shields would buckle. He decided to take the chance.

Scotty lifted a slab of metal from the wall with care. He handed it to an assistant and stared at the locked circuits to the doors of auxiliary control. Hands on his hips, leaning forward in concentration, he was the picture of frustration. Mentally he dissected the mechanics of the situation and admitted there was nothing he could do.

"The devil alone knows what's goin' on out there," he muttered, "and I can't do a thing about it! Come on, now, let go," he pleaded.

The locked circuits slipped back into place with an infinitesimal click and Scotty's face broke into a fond smile.

"I don't know why you did it," he said, "and I'll not ask."

"Scotty!"

Scotty started at the sound of the captain's voice, but answered immediately.

"Yes, sir!"

"Red alert! Get into auxiliary control! We'll run the ship from there! Prepare to return fire!"

"Aye, sir," said the engineer, already moving. He motioned his crew to assume emergency posts, Connor at the navigational controls, Sru at the phasers, and took the helm himself. "Awaiting orders, Captain."

"Good. When he comes in for another run, I want to dive under him, warp factor six, and then turn and fire on him from the rear. He thinks we're dead. If we can fool him we might be able to stop him cold! Here he comes . . . get ready, Scotty . . . now! Ahead warp six!"

"Warp six, Captain," replied Scotty as the *Enterprise* shot forward and dived under the enemy vessel. The Romulan fired, but too late, so that the blasts barely rocked the Federation starship.

"Commander! He's behind us!"

S'Talon's eyes died, but he snapped, "Turn! He will try to strike us from the rear!"

The *Enterprise*'s phasers struck just as the *Raptor* wheeled. The shot caught her across the stern and swung the ship in a dizzying spin. S'Talon clutched the wall, dimly aware of damage reports flooding the intercom. He had misjudged Kirk—as had others before him. He had not considered all the possibilities. He had given all power to the forward shields, hoping to protect the ship from a direct Federation attack, but Kirk had not been direct. The *Enterprise*'s captain had surely known the cloaking device was a power drain and surmised his enemy could protect only one side of the ship. Or he had taken the chance. At any rate, the ship was destroyed and he must now give the most difficult command of his career. He withdrew for a moment in preparation, aware his crew waited for him to order the ship's destruction. Livius, he noted with ironic satisfaction, was dead.

"Good work, Scotty!"

Kirk drew a deep breath and attacked phase two of his plan. Though he now had auxiliary control and could run the ship from there, the transporter and shuttle bays were still under Countess' influence. If he were to try to take prisoners, perhaps against their will, he would have to use the transporters.

"Countess," he said in a carefully controlled voice, "thank you. I know now that you love me. It's . . . very special. And I want to share it."

"I want you to be happy . . . but there are no others. I want to please you . . ."

There was frustration in the computer voice.

"There are others on the Romulan ship."

Countess considered this.

"Yes," it replied.

"If I could speak to them, they might be willing to beam aboard. There would be others and I would be very happy."

"You must be happy," said Countess and the stars on the main viewscreen rippled into a Romulan profile.

" . . . we will not destroy this ship!" S'Talon was saying. "The life of the empire depends upon it! We will use every means at our disposal to give the Praetor time . . ."

"Time for what, Commander?"

S'Talon whirled.

"Kirk!"

The captain smiled.

"The legendary S'Talon refuses to destroy his ship. For time. Time for what?"

"You will learn that, Captain, but too late."

"If you really wish to delay me there is a better way than dying by inches. If you and the remainder of your crew would beam aboard the *Enterprise* we could spend a great deal of time trying to discover what you are so steadfastly trying to hide."

S'Talon raised an eyebrow, so like Spock it made the doctor shiver. The Romulan aimed a look of pure challenge at Kirk.

"I accept your terms, Captain," he said.

Admiral Iota glared at the *Potemkin*'s captain. Anger seethed through him, effectually blocking his mind against words he did not wish to accept. Garson seemed completely unaware of his feelings and for that he was glad. It would have given the young captain too much power over him.

" . . . I am sorry, Admiral, but that's the way it stands. There's nothing I can do about it. My orders come directly from Star Fleet Headquarters. The *Potemkin*, with me in command, is to head the force. You will have full control of all diplomatic and intelligence contact and I am to be guided by your recommendations wherever possible . . ."

The words slid over Iota like quicksilver. He had not anticipated this. Poppaelia had forestalled any direct attempt to gain military command of the mission. He always was a conservative fool.

"You must, of course, follow orders," murmured Iota.

"That is my intention," replied Garson, comprehending more than Iota suspected.

"Still, it does no harm to be prepared. I shall personally conduct a security check on the *Potemkin*. As my flagship she will not only be a primary target but our most potent weapon."

Garson noted how easily the admiral claimed the *Potemkin,* but he answered with his usual grave courtesy.

"An excellent idea, Admiral. Your expertise will be highly valued. Lieutenant Bowetski, please escort Admiral Iota. An escort will avoid any misunderstandings over security clearance, sir."

"Thank you, Captain," Iota answered smoothly. "I'm sure we'll manage to work together."

"Yes, sir," replied Garson as the admiral turned away. He had his doubts about their ability to work together, but Iota's security inspection would keep him occupied for a while. He began to appreciate Poppaelia's warning about the ruthlessness of Iota's reactions. Not five minutes after Poppaelia's call Iota had tried to usurp military control of the mission. He had cited tactical brilliance, his special knowledge of the Romulans and his more mature years in a voice filled with tolerance for Garson's lesser status. The *Potemkin*'s captain grinned as he recalled the shock on Iota's face when Garson agreed with him and the total bewilderment in the admiral's eyes when Garson refused his offer of command.

Garson went over all he had ever heard about Iota, from official Star Fleet press releases to the idle gossip of space-weary travellers. Everything about the man—except the statistics of his life—was vague, obscure, including Poppaelia's veiled hints. Iota had no close personal friends. His life appeared to be his work and his work was Star Fleet Intelligence, his specialty the Romulans.

Garson ran a hand through his thick, pale hair. The "escort" had been a transparent ruse to keep Iota under surveillance. Garson knew he was no match for Iota in the devious field of espionage. He did not try to be. He quietly set up an honor detail from security whose job it was to continually escort the admiral. Iota's overt movements were documented while nominally paying him the compliment of an honor guard.

The *Potemkin*'s captain entered the turbo-lift, muttering "bridge" in a preoccupied voice. Garson was in his early forties, unremarkable in appearance except for the unusual clarity of his grey eyes. Most observers would have tagged him "stalwart" and thought no more about it. His close friends knew him to be completely trustworthy. He was possessed of a fair military mind, but his greatest asset was an unflinching acknowledgment of his own limitations. This and his deceptively gentle manner made him a gifted commander, for he utilized to the full the talents of those who served him. As he stepped onto the bridge, Lieutenant Arviela's small form rose from the command chair, deftly making way for him.

"Thank you, Lieutenant."

Garson's courtesy was one of the characteristics his crew found most endearing. Arviela handed him an authorization to be initialed and then resumed her customary position at the helm.

He scanned the memo and noted Poppaelia was as good as his word. Garson's authority in this special mission would go on record not only at Star Fleet Headquarters, but in the *Potemkin*'s log as well.

"How're we doing?" he asked mildly.

"On course, sir," answered Arviela.

"ETA?"

"Three point two-five hours to Starbase Eight."

Garson turned to the communications station.

"Any word from Kirk? Any intercepted Romulan transmissions?"

"Negative, sir. It's quiet."

"Too quiet. Like a tomb," muttered Garson morosely. He was trying hard not to think of the physical aspects of war, but Iota's raven-croaking prophecies hung over him. Even the stars were frail and tentative compared to the void of space between them, and human life was infinitely more fragile.

The Praetor stood on the bridge of his flagship, a royal figure in his military regalia. The Romulan fleet was assembled before him, prepared for an historic foray. It was the moment for a speech.

"My Praetor."

The Praetor glanced over his shoulder. The panic in his aide's voice was alarming.

"What is it, Pompe?"

"S'Tor is dead."

"The commander of the *Remus?* When?"

"Just a few moments ago. He was taken suddenly. He must be replaced."

"Yes. Are none of his officers qualified?"

"The *Remus* is running with half its complement now. They are key personnel. If one of them must be pulled into a position of command, it will leave a vital post unmanned."

"You will command her yourself, Pompe."

"I, my Praetor? I have no experience with that class vessel."

"We must fill the maw of necessity, Pompe. You will report directly to me. We need numbers now, not expertise. You are dismissed."

"Yes, my Praetor."

Inconvenient, thought the Praetor as Pompe backed from the room, to lose my aide—but dangerous to lose

S'Tor. It did not bode well for the coming encounter. He must move quickly or he would have no fleet to command.

"Commander."

"My Praetor."

"You may order the fleet to move out."

The commander's satanic dark eyes gleamed.

"We are ready, my Praetor."

"Four ships are to be left at the borders of the Neutral Zone to defend our backs. That rear guard will be commanded by Tiercellus. In the unlikely event that I am lost . . . you will report to him. The rest of the fleet will proceed to the planet Canara. And Commander, this is my flagship. It is to be protected at all times. A squadron of the smaller vessels will surround it. There must be no gaps in their formation."

"Yes, my Praetor. All shall be as you have commanded."

"Then," said the Praetor, "for the empire, in the name of our august and revered emperor, we will return victorious!"

"Victory!" echoed the commander.

"Victory!" shouted the bridge crew.

The Praetor smiled as the echoes of victory rose around him.

Star Fleet Intelligence Headquarters loomed stark and silent in the moonlight. The trees planted around its perimeter dappled the walls with shifting shadows. Familiar sounds of night-flying insects covered the click of Poppaelia's footsteps.

He was about to attempt burglary. He had no authority for his actions but his own unsubstantiated fears. What he proposed to do was a court-martial offense. If the building's computerized security system failed to stop him, the grinding gears of justice would, but he had to know the worst. He had exhausted every normal avenue of information without uncovering conclusive evidence of his suspicions. The only option left was a thorough search of Iota's office, but that was a touchy business. Poppaelia could ask no one to take the risk but himself.

The more he mulled over Iota's actions, the more uneasy he became. Intuition told him where the Romulans were concerned Iota was a little mad. He actually wanted to fight them, regardless of the consequences, and Poppaelia had provided him with a perfect opportunity. Poppaelia shuddered at his lack of insight and the resolution to verify his evaluations strengthened.

He moved into range of the building's security scanner and waited. A piercing red light blinded him for a moment and a computer voice demanded, "Identify!"

"Poppaelia, Arc, Rear-Admiral. Security code blue."

The computer registered this information and shot back, "Prepare for retina scan."

Poppaelia opened both eyes and willed himself not to flinch under the white light of the computer's camera eye.

"Scan affirmative. Verify code blue."

Poppaelia slipped a card into the computer slot. One of his many acquaintances had procured it for him. The man's reputation was dubious, but he had always kept a bargain, and he owed the admiral a sizable favor. If the computer accepted this coding, he would be in the clear. If not . . . he might well be dead. It was now or never.

"Security override confirmed."

The big, double doors of the building's main entrance slid open and Poppaelia stepped through them with an audible sigh of relief. He sought out Iota's office and was about to enter when he stopped short. All security in the building was supposed to be linked to the computer, but it would be like Iota to rig a special alarm for his own office. Poppaelia regarded the closed door with slitted eyes. All around the door frame ran a hairline stripe of white. For a moment he thought it was purely decorative, but on closer inspection he realized it was a cleverly concealed laser field. Anyone passing through it would be fried.

The field was neatly camouflaged, but it was a fairly simple device. Deactivating it was likely to be equally simple. Poppaelia ran his hands over the outside edge of the door frame, but found no switch. He stepped back and studied the door again, then he deliberately placed one finger on the nameplate beside it and pushed. His reward was instantaneous. The white line vanished and the doors to Iota's office slid smoothly open.

Fifteen minutes later he found what he wanted in the lower right hand drawer of Iota's locked desk. He spread a sheaf of file folders across the desk top and read their labels with growing horror. To make absolutely sure of what he was seeing, he flipped open the top file. The title page of a thick report mesmerized him. "Romulan Invasion, Plan I," he read. "Specifications: six starship class vessels, twelve reconnaissance ships and thirty cargo shuttles . . ." There were over twenty folders, each outlining a different plan for destroying the Romulan empire. Plan seventeen called for four starships and six scouts. The hairs over Poppaelia's ears tingled.

Time was running out. SICR's small but sophisticated metallic brain acknowledged this. The home it sought still eluded its sensors. Its appointed destiny was the starship *Enterprise*. Beyond that, it had no directives. It made a gradual turn, following its preprogrammed pattern. The sensors glanced off a large object, registered in SICR's memory banks and switched away from the asteroid it had identified.

The stars watched its zig-zag course with faint amusement. Their stately dance made the small computer's movements as jerky and laughable as a Chaplin comedy, yet they were not intolerant. In its way the tiny craft was fulfilling its destiny as they fulfilled theirs. It searched for its home port even as they, moving bravely into the unknown with the most rudimentary description as its guide. It was a flourish in the dance, a chuckle in the midst of splendor.

SICR kept to its course, aware only of what it lacked: the starship *Enterprise*.

Chapter 10

Tiercellus walked with stiff, measured steps toward his cabin. Though the sentries on either side of the door looked neither to the right nor the left, he knew they were aware of his every move. He must betray no weakness before them. He raised his chin defiantly as he passed between them. The moment the cabin doors closed behind him he doubled up in pain, one hand clutching his right side. He staggered as he groped for his medication and grimly willed himself to live. He was needed. He would succumb to the laws of nature only when the crisis was past.

The pain began to ease and he could breathe, though each gasp still felt as if his lungs were tearing. He walked carefully across the cabin and sank into an oversize, padded chair, gripping the arms until his knuckles went white. He closed his eyes and waited out the pain. It ebbed slowly from his body and mind.

He had been foolish, carried away by all that must be done like a raw recruit. He had neglected his medication and almost precipitated an untimely death. No more. The empire needed him. He would let the ship's physician bully him as much as she wished, even if it meant swallowing an endless array of pills and potions.

He took an experimental deep breath and was pleased to note it hurt only a little. A few more minutes and he would again be fit for duty.

"Sir."

The sentry's voice echoed in the desk communicator.

"What is it?"

"The weapons master asks to see you."

"Very well."

It took a conscious effort on Tiercellus' part to keep the fatigue from his voice. He closed his eyes, drawing on all his strength to carry him through the interview.

"My pledge is to obey."

The deep, gravelly voice brought Tiercellus to his feet—too quickly. The weapons master reached to support him.

"You are ill, my friend."

Tiercellus shook his head.

"Merely elderly, Hexce. It is of no consequence."

Hexce gently lowered his commander back into his chair. Tiercellus waved a hand toward another.

"Sit down, Hexce. I have not seen you in twenty years. I thought you must be dead."

There was a glint of humor in Tiercellus' eyes.

"Not I, sir. I am too stubborn to die."

"More likely too strong."

Tiercellus regarded the other man with undisguised affection. He and Hexce had served together for many years. They had saved each other's lives. Now they were again together for this final encounter. Somehow it was fitting.

"Your presence here is luck I did not expect. Are you willing to be my strong right arm once again? I am not sure of my own strength. Were I to drop at a crucial moment . . . Hexce, there must be someone I can trust."

Hexce's brow wrinkled. The muscles across his broad back bunched as he slammed one fist into his palm.

"Whatever you ask of me, I will do, but I am an engineer, not a leader of men."

Tiercellus smiled unexpectedly.

"You have, on occasion, led me."

Hexce chuckled.

"I have pledged to obey. If that means being obeyed . . . I accept, Commander."

"Good. We will go over the Praetor's orders together and I will tell you what I know of our young friend S'Talon. He, too, has a part to play in all of this."

"He was always a likely lad, though too honest to get ahead politically."

"At the moment, his honesty is being used against him. We will discuss the details . . ."

". . . over a glass of ale?" finished Hexce.

"You never change, Hexce. In a world as transient as ours, that is a rare thing."

"Perhaps not always a good thing. My day is over. Since our last battle, I have not found a commander I can follow with a quiet heart."

"We are two old hawks, Hexce. It is time we were returned to the forest, to die as we were bred."

Tiercellus extended his hand.

"Come, my friend. One last task and we will rest."

Hexce's massive hand closed around Tiercellus' forearm.

"For the good of the empire," he said, and the two men's eyes locked in complete understanding.

The pale sun of Canara shed its white light over fields of rippling gran. Endless winds swept the planet and they pushed and tossed the fields into waves and whitecaps, the tide changing with the direction of the wind. An ocean of gran chattered around rocky foothills and crept up the sides of towering mountains.

Romm Joramm, on his knees in the middle of a field, raised his eyes to the mountains with the clouds swirling around their peaks, and reflected that Canara had come a long way. A decade ago the view had been considerably different: unyielding rock and sand everywhere, with isolated pockets of vegetation clustered around the few natural springs. Life had been hard. Survival was the god many of his people worshipped.

But the Federation had changed all that. Not, he thought sourly, that they had gone out of their way to bring about sweeping technological advances, but they had suggested new ways of using the knowledge and tools Canara already possessed. The result had been a dramatic jump in the standard of living. Life was still hard, but now there was enough for all. Taken as a whole, he was glad he had been part of the movement to join the Federation.

Joramm rocked back on his heels and contemplated the sea of gran. Here was food for his people and health for the galaxy. Gran was a source of medicine as well as food. In unrefined gran itself or the flour milled from it, there was a powerful chemical which accounted in part for the Canarans' physical endurance and lack of disease. This much the Federation scientists had discovered and passed on to the people.

And they bought all surpluses of gran at a fair price. Yes, life was now good . . . so much for the people to learn and see. As a Canaran elder he must learn first, see first, to guide them as they stretched their minds beyond their home world. Bending the tough Canaran will was like trying to bend a steel spring—when pressure was released it immediately snapped back to its original form. That will must be bent if Canarans were to grow and live in a world populated by radically different beings. He was guilty himself of insular, archaic thinking. He sighed, letting the weight of his responsibility escape with his breath. He would worry later. Now there was much to do.

Joramm's back bent to his work once more, his rhythmic movements as he weeded the field hypnotically restful to his mind. The sun beat down on his white hair and the ripening gold he tended. A billowing wind washed the field, catching up Joramm's sigh and whirling it away with the tide.

"Livius was right. You are mad."

Argelian was beyond anger. His voice held a tired, dry certainty S'Talon found much more alarming. He doubted his ability to win Argelian over again, but the necessity of trying was inescapable.

"Argelian, we are beyond debate. We are captured. I acknowledge that to be my decision, but I will not justify it to you or any other crew member. You will accept the authority that is mine by law, or you will reap the consequences. I do not think there is a man here physically capable of stopping me if I should desire to kill you."

Argelian paled. He had never heard his commanding officer make an idle threat. He stiffened to attention and backed away. S'Talon watched him, knowing the man was cowed. He did not wish to make an enemy of

Argelian, but there was a time to assert authority. Now at all costs, he must maintain discipline.

S'Talon looked around the *Enterprise*'s detention area. Its air of freedom was created by a lack of visible sentries. The chamber was spare but comfortable. Except for the shimmering force field in the doorway, it could have been crew's quarters in any military installation.

"Centurion."

"Yes, Commander?"

"You know Argelian better than I. Do you think he will rebel?"

"No. But you may have made him an enemy."

"No man likes to be mastered. Still, it was necessary."

S'Tarleya nodded. Since the attempt on his life, she had been S'Talon's unobtrusive shadow. Now as she stood behind his chair, she noticed for the first time fatigue in his posture. He was fighting his own men as well as the enemy. Soon he would be torn apart between them. The Praetor had made him a scapegoat, counting on his sense of honor to hold him to his post. Everyone's hand was against him. Only in his centurion would he find unequivocal loyalty.

She looked down at his dark hair with its rebellious waves and her eyes softened. He felt his cause worth dying for, worth the sacrifice of his honor and his good name as well. Her motivation was less overt. As a Romulan officer, she was pledged to defend the empire, yet Tiercellus had not asked that of her. He had asked her to protect S'Talon in full confidence of her reply, and he had been wise. There was only one thing she would trade her life for: the welfare of someone she loved.

"Now, Centurion," said S'Talon, "you see the alternative I spoke of."

"Yes, Commander. I do not believe it would have occurred to me."

"You must learn to think beyond regulations, Centurion."

"I am learning it is sometimes necessary to do so," she answered.

S'Talon leaned back in his chair and closed his eyes. S'Tarleya watched as he relaxed and was humbled by his trust in her. Let all the others betray him. She would not be an agent of his destruction.

Yang pushed the remains of his lunch into the disposal unit and regarded his desk. Tapes in boxes of fifty were stacked around its perimeter. Loose tapes littered the work area. He had spent the past week on inventory and he still had three hundred boxes to check. The tapes were reproduced in triplicate and each set required his personal authorization. The next time some overstuffed line officer made a derogatory remark about administrators he would just give them a tour and let them use their expensive, precise scientific training on his kind of detail. He judged they would be near a nervous breakdown in three days. The thought gave him infinite satisfaction as he reached for the next tape.

"Commodore."

Damn. He had just revved himself up to impulse power. All he needed was some idiotic diplomatic dispute.

"I thought I told you not to disturb me."

"Yes, sir, but I have Admiral Iota, from Star Fleet Headquarters, here, sir. And Captain Garson of the *Potemkin*."

"Well, show them in!"

Yang rose to his feet with anything but grace—tapes

sliding off the table and tangling up his feet—as Iota marched into the room.

"Yang, what have you done about the Romulan situation?" demanded the admiral.

"I am making some discreet inquiries, sir. As yet nothing has come of them, but given time . . ."

"We don't have time! The Romulan fleet will invade Federation space and we'll be sitting here waiting for answers."

"Have you heard from Kirk, Commodore?"

Yang turned at the sound of the firm, reserved voice and took a good look at Captain Garson. He had not met the man before. Garson's steadfast attitude, platinum hair and grey eyes combined with his height created an impression of quiet competence. He liked him.

"No. Normal communications are still blocked and, since you ask the question, I assume other, less obvious communication lines are also inoperative."

Garson inclined his head. A man of few words, thought Yang. Admirable. He was surrounded by words and they made him tired.

"However, I am working on another method of contacting the *Enterprise* . . . at the moment I can't disclose how . . . "

"Commodore, I am a member of the Star Fleet Defense Council and I have full security clearance. I demand to know what means . . . "

"It would be a breach of faith, sir. Besides, isn't it your theory the *Enterprise* is destroyed?"

Iota stopped short.

"Yes."

"Then why waste time on an attempt to contact a nonexistent vessel?"

Garson's eyes flickered with interest. Yang was more than he looked.

144

"Of course, of course . . . at any rate our primary purpose is to discover what is going on out there. Since there are no new developments, I propose we take our ships across the Romulan Neutral Zone into the heart of the Romulan empire, to the horse's mouth, so to speak. If we move first we may prevent a galactic war. Commodore, you will provide us with the most direct route to the planet Romulus."

Yang's eyes goggled. There were no gaps in Iota's logic: it was a tangled knot pulled tight, destruction in every loop. He collected his wits.

"No."

Garson's statement was simple, clear and sensible. Yang relaxed.

"Admiral, you must know entry into the Neutral Zone is, in the eyes of both the Romulans and the Federation, an act of war," Yang managed.

Iota opened his mouth, but Garson cut in.

"You are right, Commodore," he answered smoothly. "The only alternative is to patrol the zone."

"Useless toadhopping! Where has it gotten us?"

"I'll tell you where it hasn't gotten us, Admiral. It hasn't gotten us into a war." Yang had control now and was pushing for all he was worth. "I live with the 'Romulan threat' you talk about. I've learned the quickest way to turn a threat into reality is to challenge it. Sit back, watch, and the threat usually fades away. I don't mean we should bury our heads in the sand, but asking for a fight is the surest way I know to get one."

"I concur. Entering the Neutral Zone comes under my jurisdiction as military commander of this detachment. We will not violate the Neutral Zone unless directly provoked," stated Garson.

Iota smoldered. For a moment Garson was afraid he would try to pull rank and the situation would become ugly, but he thought better of it.

"Then we will patrol the Zone, gentlemen, and bide our time. But under my protest. I will accept no responsibility for the decision."

And you will get none, thought Yang.

"Departure in one hour," stated Iota. "Until that time I will be in my quarters. Gentlemen."

Yang and Garson watched the admiral's strategic retreat. The doors closed behind him and Yang turned to the captain.

"Sit down, Captain. Can I get you something? No? Then answer one question for me. How in the name of all that's holy did that idiot get command of this mission? He's just about sent a formal challenge to the Romulan fleet."

"How did he ever make admiral? Or get assigned to the Defense Council?" countered Garson. "It's my understanding he's cultivated friends."

Yang smiled.

"He should have gone directly into politics. He missed his calling. Can you control him?"

"I don't have to, Commodore. I am in full military command of the mission."

"Oh yes you do. You may have a perfectly legal authorization from Star Fleet Command, but on the borders of the Neutral Zone you're a long way from headquarters. You know the kind of problems he could cause just by opening his mouth."

"I admit there is a danger."

"Sir, you are a master of understatement. I hope you've considered all the ramifications."

"I have."

"Then let me just say that the welfare of the Federation is close to my heart. I've spent twenty years keeping the threads of communication between the Romulan empire and the Federation unbroken. It's a tenuous thread and the slightest jar is capable of snapping it. Iota isn't a jar, he's a fusion bomb. If any of us are to survive, peace is the only way and the only hope for peace is to get to know and understand each other's motives. We can't do that if we can't talk. Right now our contact with the Romulans comes mainly from neutral traders and the barest bit of automated intelligence sensing. That's indirect enough. I don't want that thread snapped. I simply wish to make my position clear. You understand me, Captain?"

"I believe I do, Commodore."

Yes, Yang was more than he appeared, and this offer of support was something he had not counted on. It was a bonus that might make all the difference.

"Thank you, Commodore."

Garson smiled as he left, surprising Yang with the warmth it lent his face. This man was a gift from the gods, but still Yang could not shake a feeling of gathering darkness. He turned back to his inventory tapes, knowing if the galaxy exploded tomorrow it was still his job to finish checking them today.

The *Potemkin*'s VIP cabin was dim, an artificial twilight which accented a circular port set into the ceiling showing the changing panorama of the constellations. Iota, stretched out on the bed, found them anything but comforting. He closed his eyes to shut them out and found himself thinking of Kirk and the Romulans. Of all the commanders in the fleet, Kirk had managed to engage the Romulans twice. His ship had been the first to actually see a Romulan face to face . . . and they had looked like Vulcans!

Iota remembered his shock at that news, almost a thrill. He had read Kirk's log entries and Commander Spock's paper on that first encounter with avid interest. Spock had postulated the Romulans to be offshoots of the Vulcan race and Iota had been quick to grasp the significance of this. He envied both Kirk and Spock their opportunities to match wits with such an adversary.

He tried to remember when he first realized the Romulans were the ultimate challenge in the game of power. He must have been very young. His father had been an armchair admiral who channeled his military aspirations into war games. Some of Iota's pleasantest childhood memories centered around the game table as he and his father waged sham battles across lucite space. Even then he had always wanted to fight the Romulans—or better yet, be them! The Klingons were dangerous, but distressingly repetitious, and the Andorians too flighty for a real contest. Only the Romulans made the game worthwhile.

All his life he had played at strategy second- and even third-hand. Now he was about to make the game a reality. He would have his own chance at a glorious contest. For once he would be using all of his abilities, using them to save the Federation from its own blindness. When the debris of battle was cleared away, he would be revealed as the hero whose insight and ability had saved the day. From childhood he had prepared for this opportunity and he was not about to let a lot of bureaucratic red tape get in the way. Poppaelia, Garson, Yang—they were all fools. He had always known the Romulans would eventually take on the Federation. War was in their blood. If the cooing doves could not recognize an act of war, he could, and he would save them in spite of themselves.

Kirk strode purposefully out of his cabin. Intent on the problem of making S'Talon talk, he narrowly missed colliding with his first officer.

"Sorry, Spock," he apologized. "I was preoccupied."

"That was apparent, Captain. Perhaps with the

same problem which brings me here."

"The Romulans?"

"Yes."

"You've been talking with them. Found any weak spots?"

"Possibly. I do not believe the crew are aware of the reason for their commander's actions. They are uneasy about him. One of the sentries even reported an open confrontation between S'Talon and a crew member."

"He stands completely alone, then?"

"No. He has a personal guard, or aide. She seems to be totally loyal."

"She?"

Spock nodded.

"What does she look like?"

Spock cocked an eyebrow.

"She has no distinguishing characteristics."

"Spock, is she attractive?"

"I believe you would find her so."

"And totally devoted to S'Talon . . ."

Kirk's eyes became distant.

"Spock, I think we have our lever. Get S'Talon and this aide to briefing room two. How much do they know about Vulcans?"

"I would say approximately what we know of them."

"The bare essentials. It just might . . . work."

Kirk's reflective mood changed abruptly.

"Go on, Spock. And Spock . . . try to look ruthless."

"Captain?"

"Never mind. Just don't say anything. That'll do. And follow my lead. Whatever they're hiding must be big or they wouldn't have gone to such lengths to conceal it."

"Surrender is not a part of the Romulan outlook. I

149

agree with you. Moreover, what they wish to conceal must be of paramount importance to the Federation."

"Why us?"

"They were on our side of the Neutral Zone."

"Good point. And from what S'Talon said, time is on their side."

"Then we must make haste."

"Indeed we must. Bring them."

Chapter 11

"Captain's Log: stardate three-one two-seven point two.

"With the release of auxiliary control the computer seems to have detached itself from active involvement. It is allowing repairs and it has accepted a cursory reprogramming of the personnel files. Though the ship is still being run through auxiliary control, and will require a starbase facility for a complete overhaul, it is estimated the bridge will be operational in twenty-four hours. The Romulans have given us little trouble but we have made no progress in discovering their purpose on this side of the Neutral Zone."

Briefing Room Two was an armed camp. S'Talon and his centurion, seated opposite Kirk and his officers, were maintaining a solid shield of distrust. Kirk parried and fenced, discovering more of S'Talon's caliber with each stroke. It was a stalemate, with each side holding its own. Kirk glanced at his first officer. Spock was observing the situation in silence, his face impassive, his arms folded.

"Mister Spock," said the captain, "how can we convince our adversaries of our trustworthiness? Their attitude reveals a distressing lack of confidence."

"Indeed, Captain, short of telepathic contact I can think of no logical course of action."

"You would use your power in this manner, Vulcan?"

The centurion's voice was hard and S'Talon's surprise showed clearly in his expression. Spock remained silent, watching the Romulans with emotionless objectivity.

"Kirk, you will not permit this?"

"I am afraid, Commander, we must use every means at our disposal to discover your purpose. If it requires Vulcan mental techniques . . . the choice is yours, Commander."

S'Talon's eyes narrowed as he faced Kirk in grim silence. There was anger in them, dark and dangerous.

"Spock."

Kirk's voice hung in the air, the soft intonation a striking contrast to its ominous import.

"Come, Centurion," said Spock.

S'Talon was on his feet, his fist slamming down on the table.

"No! If someone is to endure this barbarism it will be me! I will not have my crew subjected to torture!"

Two security guards stepped forward but Kirk held S'Talon with his eyes.

"Centurion," repeated Spock.

S'Talon started to speak but the centurion cut him off.

"It is my privilege to serve the empire, Commander."

She rose, her movements lending feminine grace to the severe lines of her uniform. She strode toward the door, head high. Spock turned to follow her. The deliberation of his movements made S'Talon shudder. He knew only too well the terrifying effects of a forced mind link.

Kirk had not taken his eyes from S'Talon's face. He regretted the pain he was causing, but the Romulan was stubborn. "Now, Commander," he said, "we will continue our discussion."

As the doors closed behind Spock the centurion turned to face him. He admired her control, the light of challenge which covered the fear in her eyes, the defensive attitude she had adopted.

"I warn you, I will resist."

Spock knew that to be true, knew also she was fully aware of her danger. Obviously such extremity was used by the Romulans, though they had not expected violence from a Vulcan. Her courage in the face of mental torture was remarkable. He paid tribute to it.

"That will not be necessary, Centurion."

At her complete surprise he elaborated.

"The Federation does not employ torture as a method of interrogation."

"A trick!"

"Yes."

"No!" she said and sprang toward the door.

Spock caught her, carefully keeping her hands away from his face as she struggled and fought in his grasp.

"No!" she panted. "You will force him into betrayal! He will sacrifice his honor for nothing! No!! No!"

She realized she could not overpower Spock and stopped fighting, raising dark, swimming eyes to his.

"Please. Do not do this. There must be another way. I will speak! Do not force him to betray himself!"

Spock regarded her with compassion.

"And what of your honor?" he asked curiously.

"It does not matter. I will speak! But stop this!"

"As you wish, Centurion."

S'Talon studied the Terran captain, trying to probe his depths. All he knew of Kirk—his personal brilliance, military genius and diplomatic flair—warned him to proceed with care. He vowed not to underestimate the man again, though he had always heard Terrans were weaklings.

"So, Commander, once again I'll ask you . . . what are you doing in Federation space?"

"It is sufficient that I am here. I await the legal proceedings for my execution."

Kirk's voice was sharp, intense.

"There will be no execution . . . for you. As for your crew . . ."

"They expect no other fate," said the commander. "That is our way."

"Really, Commander? Then why are they even now buying their lives . . . with cooperation?"

Kirk caught the quick flinch of surprise and pain on S'Talon's face and decided to press his advantage.

"You lie," said S'Talon, his voice grating. "Humans are well-known liars."

"Perhaps. But this time I have no need to lie. They betray you. Why should you sacrifice your life for them? Even your centurion is vulnerable."

S'Talon's eyes blazed.

"She will say nothing voluntarily, Captain. She has been with me for years! She is a loyal officer!"

"But she is also a woman . . . a very attractive woman. I don't think Spock will have to use force."

"No!" snarled S'Talon.

"She went with him willingly . . ." murmured Kirk, placing a definite, soft emphasis on the last word.

"As a Romulan officer! She volunteered for this mission though she knew it would mean her death! She would die to save her people!"

" 'To save her people,' " repeated Kirk. " 'The life of the empire' . . . you meant that literally. Of course—why else would the Romulans risk a galactic war? It would be suicide unless . . . unless death without the risk was certain."

S'Talon's face had become cold, the skin across his prominent cheekbones taut. Only his eyes revealed his emotions and they were full of despairing anger. Kirk continued his speculations.

"You were the decoy! You kept outsiders from interfering! That's why you used the cloaking device to such an extent, why you let your ship be destroyed rather than seek escape . . . to buy time! But time for what! Tell me, Commander!"

Kirk suddenly realized S'Talon was not listening to him. The Romulan's eyes were fixed on a point beyond Kirk and they had grown wide with horror. Keeping a wary eye on his adversary, Kirk turned just as Spock announced, "Captain, I have summoned Doctor McCoy. The centurion collapsed."

Spock held her in his arms, her limp form and pallor making her appear frighteningly delicate. The captain's surprise was obvious, but S'Talon did not see it. His eyes were for the centurion alone.

"Even Klingons would not have done this!" he spat.

Spock ignored the venom in S'Talon's voice. For all the reaction he made it might have been the most civil of pleasantries. He carefully placed the centurion on the floor and rose to face the impassioned Romulan.

"Commander, the centurion revealed nothing but her loyalty before she collapsed. I did not invade her mind nor harm her physically."

"We do not employ torture," contributed Kirk.

S'Talon knelt by S'Tarleya, his eyes on her face.

"You tricked me, Kirk?"

"Yes, Commander. The centurion's collapse is unfortunate, but I assure you Mister Spock is in no way responsible for her condition."

S'Talon looked up at Spock, whose whole attitude expressed his concern.

"I believe you. This was not unexpected."

Kirk and his first officer exchanged a mystified look.

McCoy, medical kit in his hand, threaded his way between Kirk, Spock and S'Talon to kneel beside the centurion. He ran his scanner over her, grasped her neck and gently lifted her head, then eased her back to the floor. With clinical thoroughness he studied her face. The arched eyebrows and dark lashes were like figures painted on startlingly white paper, framed in the black mass of her hair. He glanced at the Romulan commander. S'Talon looked both resigned and grieved.

"Bones, what is it?"

McCoy drew his eyes from the Romulan's face and looked up at Kirk.

"It's myrruthesia. Peculiar to Vulcans and Romulans, but generally very rare and communicable only in its early stages. This seems to be a more virulent strain. . . . I can't tell just yet how dangerous it is . . ."

"I can." S'Talon's voice was like gravel. "The centurion will die within forty-eight hours if the antidote is not administered. It may even now be too late to save her."

"The antidote?"

"Quinneal, Jim. But what kind of effect it has on this mutated form of the virus, I don't know." McCoy administered an injection before orderlies took the centurion to sickbay. "You'd better come along, too,

156

Mister Spock, Commander. We have a small supply of preventive vaccine aboard."

"We will be there shortly, Doctor."

Spock's answer made it plain he would appear in his own good time.

"See that you do, Mister Spock."

McCoy was about to say something more but he caught the look Kirk aimed at him and turned to follow the centurion's gurney as it was propelled out the door.

"Is that what you're trying to hide, Commander? Illness? A plague that threatens the entire Romulan empire? But McCoy said it's communicable only in the early stages . . ."

"As the doctor surmised, this is a mutated form of the disease. It is highly contagious . . . and quinneal is not entirely successful in its prevention or cure," said S'Talon tightly.

"I still don't understand why you tried to hide the disease. The Federation might be able to help . . ."

A bitter smile tugged at S'Talon's mouth.

"Help your enemies, Captain? In a way you already are."

"The Federation and the Romulan empire may be political enemies, Commander, but we have no desire to see your people ravaged by a plague. At least we can supply medicine and our research staff here on the *Enterprise* will work on an improved vaccine."

The commander's smile deepened.

"Quinneal is created by using a distillation of gran as a catalyst. The nearest major source of gran is the Canara solar system . . . in Federation space," commented Spock.

Kirk's eyes widened, then narrowed as his mind locked on to the situation.

"The Romulan fleet is at Canara! You were to give them time to get the gran! Commander, that may not

157

be easy—not even for the Romulan fleet. The Canarans are a warrior race, simple but dangerous. They are capable of destroying the gran rather than allow it to fall into Romulan hands."

"We will do what is necessary, Captain, to save our people."

"If you try to use force against the Canarans you may destroy your people! Listen to me, Commander! It may be true that humans are liars, but Vulcans are not! Spock!"

"The captain speaks the truth, Commander. The Canarans are severe and violent, prone to extremes. They are also intensely loyal to the Federation. If you attempt to force them to refine gran for you they are quite capable of destroying the entire crop."

The taut muscles along S'Talon's jaw relaxed and he sat down, defeat undermining his military bearing.

"Then we are doomed. I have lived to see the destruction of the Romulan empire, not by military holocaust, but in this insidious arena of death commanded by a microscopic executioner."

"Commander, let us help you! The Federation does not want to lose Canara, nor does it relish an all-out war with the Romulan empire! You must trust me, Commander!"

S'Talon raised his eyes to Kirk's earnest face.

"Trust you, Captain? When you have just tricked me?"

"I admit I'm asking a lot, but the stakes are high. You have to trust me. We have to trust each other or see both sides destroyed. Hundreds of thousands of innocent lives sacrificed because of our inability to trust each other. With your help the chances of averting a galactic Armageddon are small. Without it they are non-existent."

"It seems I have little alternative, Captain."

S'Talon's shoulders straightened, accepting yet another untravelled course of action. Tiercellus had told him he must be open to new ideas, even from an enemy. His old commander had been something of a prophet.

The communications center of Star Fleet Command Headquarters was designed to handle more than two thousand simultaneous messages. Its capabilities were enormous. It served as a relay center for all military communications and not a few civilian transmissions as well. It was a round-the-clock operation, accepting, decoding and forwarding messages. The center's complexity and cold mechanical efficiency were overwhelming. Poppaelia was a little depressed by it.

Since his unauthorized expedition he had haunted communications. He knew he was driving the technicians crazy, but the confirmation of his suspicions placed him in a difficult position. He could not share his illegally gained information, nor could he produce any justifiable reason for a formal search of Iota's office and quarters. He knew the Federation had never been nearer war than at this moment, but there was nothing he could do about it. If he tried to warn Garson and Yang more directly than he already had, his credibility would be in jeopardy. He was forced to know and do nothing except check every bit of code from the Romulan sector. Three or four messages the computer had picked up were in a new cipher and this added to his worries.

He turned wearily away from a viewscreen and rubbed his bloodshot eyes. He had to rest, but not for long.

"Bryan, I'm taking a nap. Keep your eyes on those screens and your ears open. Wake me if anything—and I mean the faintest suspicion—looks unusual."

"Yes, sir," answered the communications engineer.

Poppaelia put his head on his arms. Within moments he was snoring lightly.

"Excellency."

The Praetor inclined his head.

"Excellency, we have not been able to make contact with the Canarans. The planet seems to be ruled by a council of elders, their leader being a certain Romm Joramm. We are told he is unavailable until the fifth hour, when he will return from the fields for a meal."

"Is there no means of contacting this man before that time? Have they no system of communication for emergencies?"

"Yes, but they refuse to use it. They are a literal people and I could not convince them of our need without giving them an impression of weakness."

"I will show them need! We could level the collection of hovels they call a capital with one blast. We will take what we need."

"My Praetor, I understand your feelings, but Canara not only has the largest crop of gran in the quadrant, it has the ability to refine it. If we can secure the Canarans' help we can obtain quinneal a thousand times faster than if we refined it ourselves. They understand the process—they may be primitive in some ways, but they do know how to make quinneal. Good quality, too. But we will have to be careful. They are loyal to the Federation. As yet they do not realize who we are. If we are careful we may be able to obtain the entire crop."

"They have an adequate harvest?"

"Yes. I have seen the fields. They are rich and ready to be cut. In the south the harvest has already begun."

"Speak, then, with this Romm Joramm. Offer him anything you must to get the drug."

"Excellency, I have been informed Romm Joramm

160

will speak only with the leader of the party. I think you will have to speak with him yourself."

"You will act in my behalf. How will these primitives know the difference?"

"I do not know, my Praetor, but they do. And they will deal only with you. They are shrewd, these Canarans."

"Go, then, and arrange a meeting with this man. We will speak with him, but if he does not cooperate we will take what we need . ... in the name of the Emperor."

"Yes, my Praetor."

The Praetor turned his attention to the fleet, now in orbit around Canara. The impression of strength they created was a sham. Not one ship carried a full crew. Since they left Romulus over one hundred crewmen had fallen sick. There was no time for negotiation, for diplomacy. A tiny edge of fear was growing in the Praetor's heart.

"Red alert! Red alert!"

The raucous sound of a siren flooded the *Potemkin*. The crew scrambled for battle stations.

"Enemy vessels ahead, Captain. They appear to be Klingon design, but I'll wager they're Romulan. The alliance . . ."

"Yes, Mister Farrell. Range?"

"Extreme range, sir. They seem to be holding position on the borders of the Neutral Zone."

"They do not respond to our attempts to contact them. All universal hailing frequencies . . . ineffective, sir."

"There, Garson. Are you satisfied? Four Romulan ships. Now do you believe the Federation is under attack?"

Iota's voice was cold with satisfaction.

"I will not jump to conclusions, Admiral. Those

ships—Romulan or Klingon—have not crossed the borders of the Neutral Zone. They are completely within their rights. Don't misunderstand me. We're on alert status and we'll stay there as long as those ships are in sight. Helm, bring us into position opposite the enemy vessels. Ensign, keep trying to contact them."

The *Potemkin* and her sister ships eased into position opposite the Romulans. The two fleets eyed one another but neither gave way.

"No response from the alien vessels, Captain."

"Well, do something, Garson!"

"I am, Admiral. I am waiting."

"For what? To be shot as we stand? For the Lord's sake, man, issue an ultimatum!"

"To what end?"

"The defense of the Federation!"

"Sometimes the best defense is patience. Ensign, try to monitor the alien's communications. Helm, hold position. Instruct the rest of the fleet to do the same."

Garson leaned back in the command chair and closed his eyes. He could feel Iota's frustration, a volcano under pressure. Calmly he assessed the situation. They were evenly matched. With the scout vessels the Federation fleet even had a slight advantage. However, if the Romulans—and Romulan he surmised them to be—fired on them from the Neutral Zone it would be hard to prove who was at fault. He must be extremely careful.

"Sir, the alien vessels seem to be maintaining communications silence. There's no sub-space activity at all."

"Curious. It looks like a stall. But why?"

"I'll tell you why," answered the admiral. "Can't you see that the Romulan fleet has invaded the Federation?"

"That would be the obvious motive. But we have no proof and I cannot move on suspicion."

"Sir, a message coming in. It's from the alien, sir."

"Put it on the main viewscreen."

A Romulan appeared on the screen. His close-cropped hair framed a proud and patrician face. Though well past his physical prime, his strength of will was apparent in every feature. Behind him was a rank of the exclusive Praetorian guard.

"Federation starship. In the name of the Emperor withdraw from the area or face the consequences."

"This is Captain Garson, commanding the United Space Ship *Potemkin*. Identify yourself, sir."

The grim line of the Romulan's mouth curled in contempt.

"That you may know your executioner, earthling. I am Tiercellus, Supreme Commander of the Fleet."

"What is your purpose, Tiercellus?"

The use of his name was an effective bit of insolence. Garson rose a notch in the Romulan's estimation.

"My purpose does not concern you," he answered.

"Oh, but it does. Particularly since you see fit to challenge us."

"And I repeat the challenge, Captain. Leave the area immediately. I am through bandying words."

"You are in a poor position to deliver threats. What is your reason for this confrontation? You risk a galactic war."

"I am not answerable to you. Clear the area or we will open fire."

"I don't think so. We are, if you will check your instruments, out of your range. In order for your fire to be effective you will have to cross into Federation space . . . and I don't think you're going to do that—at least not yet. You are checkmated, sir."

The Romulan's expression did not change.

"You have been warned, Captain Garson."

The viewscreen rippled and the alien ships reappeared, menacing gray bodies hovering like vultures. The analogy made an involuntary shiver crawl across Garson's shoulders.

"Captain Garson, if you do not take action against the Romulan menace, I will be forced to report your actions."

"Admiral, I will not enter the Neutral Zone, nor will I attack an enemy who wages war with words."

"If you would attack first and worry about protocol later, you would be victor. You don't seem to realize that in war there are no rules."

"And you do not seem to realize that there is as yet no war."

"Garson, you're a fool."

"Possibly. That remains to be seen."

"I consider your actions unacceptable."

"I am dealing with an entirely military situation. That area is not under your jurisdiction," Garson pointed out.

"We'll see about that. Rank has its privileges. As Chief of Intelligence, I am in an enviable position to make sure the facts of the matter appear."

Garson ignored the admiral's blathering and closed his eyes again. With every faculty he possessed he reached out for an answer.

Chapter 12

"Captain's Log: stardate thirty-one twenty-eight point six.

"The *Enterprise* is proceeding to Canara to act as intermediary between the Romulan empire and the Canarans. Communications are still inoperative, but should be repaired within the hour. We have had no contact with Star Fleet Command. Commander S'Talon has agreed to help us try to convince the Romulan leaders it is in the Federation's best interest to help them. His only concern seems to be the welfare of his people. The centurion is still in sickbay and, in spite of all Doctor McCoy can do, her condition is worsening."

Kirk sat in the doctor's office. In one hand he held McCoy's report on myrruthesia. He looked up from it, appalled by the swiftness and agony of the disease.

"Bones, isn't there anything you can do?"

"I don't think so, Jim."

The pain in McCoy's voice sent a ripple of sorrow through the captain.

"One thing we have done. Using the centurion's blood and tissue samples we've managed to isolate the mutated virus and I think we've got a quinneal derivative that will stop it cold—up to the crisis period. But it won't help the centurion . . . the disease was just too far advanced . . . I think she knew she had it when she volunteered for this mission."

"S'Talon said as much."

Both men's eyes went to the stoic figure of S'Talon bending over the centurion's bed. Framed by the doorway of the doctor's office, it was a timeless portrait of grief. A profound sadness mantled McCoy's face and the captain's eyes were dark with sympathy.

"She loves him, Jim."

"I know. S'Talon said she'd been with him for years, but I don't think he knows. It's a shame she couldn't have that at least."

"She's been delirious these last few hours—slipping in and out of sanity—and she's talked a little. S'Talon's an unusual man. Comes from an old family, well-educated and managed to stay free of the intrigues of the Romulan court. The Praetor doesn't like him."

"That explains why he was chosen as a decoy. He could be relied on to carry out the mission but his loss would be welcome. He seems to be in no man's land, in as much danger from his superiors as he is from the Federation."

"From the way she talked, more. He was almost assassinated on this mission."

Kirk's eyes shifted to the Romulan commander.

"Bones, I have a feeling S'Talon is the lever we need to push things our way."

S'Talon was unaware of Kirk and McCoy. He guarded the centurion's bedside, fiercely protective. The depth of his feeling was a surprise he did not try to analyze. He examined the pale face before him, noticed the delicacy of upswept eyebrows, the curling length of lashes, the hair spread across the pillow like a dark cloud. He smiled thinly as his centurion opened haunted black eyes.

"Commander . . ." she whispered.

"Ssshhh . . ." said S'Talon, silencing her with two gentle fingers against her lips. "Ssshhh . . ." he repeated. "I know you revealed nothing . . . or perhaps something of great value—your loyalty," he said.

Full lashes fluttered as the centurion's eyes widened in surprise.

"I could not let you betray yourself, Commander," she answered.

"I know."

"Commander . . ."

"Do not speak."

"I must. It is selfish, I know, but I want to tell you before I go . . . I have always loved you."

Obscure facets of S'Tarleya's personality coalesced for S'Talon. He had thought her loyalty unusual and valued it. Now he knew its source.

"I have been blind, Centurion. And a fool."

"Not blind. Dedicated, I think. You had no time for my love. I would have waited until you did. A fool? Maybe. For it seems you must have seen my feelings."

"Sometimes, Centurion, one holds the greatest treasure in one's hand and knows it only by its most prosaic characteristics. Familiarity is a most effective disguise."

"And now it is too late . . . for both of us."

Regret clouded S'Talon's thoughts and poured pain into the centurion's eyes. He pulled himself up short. Time enough for self-pity later. S'Talon allowed his fingers to caress her face, his touch gentle with understanding. He closed his eyes and concentrated on attaining peace. The barriers in his mind melted away.

"S'Tarleya," he thought and she turned toward him, wonder growing in her eyes. "We have this time," his mind said. "It takes little time to say . . . 'I love you.' "

"My love will be with you always," she answered.

S'Talon felt a white light wash through his mind, flooding it with crystal clarity. His perceptions were heightened. He understood with a depth and breadth he had never before reached.

"I love you, S'Tarleya," he repeated, "I love you."

From McCoy's office the two humans kept their prisoner under observation while allowing him a certain amount of privacy.

"That's what's in store for the Romulan empire, Jim: pain and loss and lingering grief," said McCoy.

Kirk studied the alien commander and his officer. Neither the centurion's helplessness nor the commander's tender strength was lost on him. The centurion was dying. They all knew it. His own impotence made him angry. In so many ways S'Talon reminded him of Spock. He had the same control, the same quiet logic. He was the kind of man the Federation needed within the Romulan empire, a man of foresight and daring who might be persuaded to consider new ideas. He was losing not only a loyal and trusted companion, but what even an outsider could see was a special kind of love. Kirk thought of disease, hopeless and final, striking the *Enterprise*. If this had happened to his ship, his world . . . Spock, Bones, Scotty, Chekov, Uhura, Sulu . . . all four hundred and thirty crew members . . . it would be intolerable.

"Bones, there must be something!"

"Research is promising, Jim, but without large quantities of refined quinneal we won't have a chance to win. Jim . . . I know how you feel, but are you sure this is the right course? The Romulans have always been our enemies . . . you know there are going to be some who will say that if we had let the empire die we'd have let a big headache die with it."

Kirk smiled wryly.

"I know. I expect a lot of flack in that area. But if we don't do something about this . . . well, as far as I'm concerned there's no other course to take. It might even be the first step in making enemies friends."

He activated the intercom.

"Spock," he said.

"Spock here."

"ETA with the planet Canara, Mister Spock?"

"Four point two-three hours, Captain. We have picked up a remote communications drone. It is of singular design and seems to be programmed by voice print. It will open only at your command."

"All right, Mister Spock. S'Talon and I will meet you in Control. Kirk out."

He walked slowly over to S'Talon, loath to intrude. The Romulan's mail tunic glittered and Kirk let himself be fascinated by it for a moment before he spoke.

"Commander . . ."

"Yes, Captain. I heard. I am ready. The centurion," he said, turning to Kirk, "is dead."

"I am sorry, Commander," said Kirk, his hazel eyes searching S'Talon's face. "Commander . . ."

The captain placed one hand on the Romulan's shoulder and S'Talon raised his eyes to Kirk's. For a timeless instant Terran and Romulan understood one another.

"Let's go," said Kirk softly.

They walked in silence to the turbo-lift, each man absorbed in his own thoughts.

"Deck eight," said Kirk as the doors slid together.

"You realize, Captain, this will not be easy. The

Praetor will believe you murdered the centurion and brainwashed me. You must convince him and his officers that is not the case. You are going into terrible danger."

"And you, Commander? You risk your life. Isn't peace—no matter how uneasy—worth the risk?"

S'Talon gauged Kirk for the hundredth time.

"Yes."

"Report, Mister Spock," announced the captain as he and S'Talon stepped into auxiliary control, now manned by the bridge crew. S'Talon's left eyebrow rose in surprise at the small control area and Kirk smiled to himself, pleased he was able to keep the Romulan from prolonged observation of the *Enterprise*'s bridge.

"Communications have been restored, sir. The computer detached the sub-space monitor, but we were able to rig a by-pass," said Uhura.

S'Talon chuckled.

"We needn't have worried about communications, then. You do not know the time I wasted on that."

"Captain."

Spock's tone definitely indicated he wished to speak privately.

"I recommend you open the communications drone before contacting Star Fleet."

Spock held out the little cube for the captain's inspection. The letters "SICR" were stenciled on one side, followed by the Federation emblem. Kirk fingered the tiny struts that made it a maneuverable spacecraft.

"This is new."

"Indeed, Captain. It is an experimental model."

"Another one?" Kirk raised the box to eye level. "This is James T. Kirk, SC 937-0176 CEC, commanding the USS *Enterprise*."

A metallic click issued from the depths of the container and the top portion opened to reveal a message tape.

"Open sesame," murmured Spock, and the captain looked startled. He handed the tape to Uhura, who slipped it into a decoding slot. Kirk, hunched over the viewer, absorbed the message. When he turned back to face Spock and S'Talon it was obvious the news had not been good.

"It's from Yang. Four starship class vessels, under the joint command of Admiral Iota and Captain Garson are on their way to the Neutral Zone to investigate our disappearance. Admiral Iota believes the *Enterprise* destroyed. He has practically sent a declaration of war to the Romulan empire. Garson is trying to hold him. Uhura, contact Star Fleet Command. Tell them . . ."

"Before you do that, Captain, you should know that there are four Romulan ships of the line guarding the Neutral Zone. They have orders to protect our escape route at all costs."

"Damn! It's like begging for a war! Uhura, contact Star Fleet Command."

Uhura turned to the tiny communications panel, her fingers flying as she attempted to contact Star Fleet.

"I have them, sir. It's Admiral Poppaelia."

"Put him on the screen."

Poppaelia's familiar face filled the small screen.

"Kirk! Thank God. What's going on out there? And a Romulan? Aboard the *Enterprise?* Why haven't you been in touch?"

"We had some mechanical difficulties, sir. I won't go into them now. I just got a special message that a detachment under Captain Garson and Admiral Iota is on its way to the Neutral Zone. Admiral, you've got to stop them!"

"I can't. They've arrived. And they've contacted the enemy. Right now they're sitting, just out of range, on the border of the Neutral Zone. On the other side of

171

the border are four Romulan ships. Stalemate. What's going on?"

"Sir, the Romulan fleet has invaded Federation space, but not for any military purpose."

Poppaelia's eyes carried a look of innocent disbelief and Kirk plunged on.

"Sir, you are aware the Romulans have been oddly insular lately." Poppaelia nodded. "We have discovered the entire population is being ravaged by disease."

"That is correct," contributed Spock. "The Romulans have been attacked by a virulent strain of myrruthesia. It is a rare virus, but it could be a major threat to Vulcan as well."

"Get McCoy up here," Kirk whispered in an aside to the communications officer.

"That still doesn't explain why the Romulans have invaded Federation space . . . did you say the entire Romulan fleet?"

"Yes. The only known cure for the disease is a substance which uses a refined form of gran as a catalyst. As you know, the Romulans are poor— especially agriculturally. They simply do not have the facilities to produce enough of this catalyst. And they are desperate. Over a third of the population has been destroyed by the disease. So they have invaded the Federation to try to buy or take enough gran to stop the plague."

"This is true?"

S'Talon nodded.

"But why didn't they appeal to the Federation for help? In a situation like this . . ."

"Pride, Admiral," answered S'Talon, "coupled with the firm conviction you would relish the destruction of the empire."

"There are many who would," admitted Poppaelia.

"What do you want me to do, Kirk? It's become a military situation. All that has to happen is for one shot to be fired and we'll be in the middle of a galactic war."

"Stop Iota." Kirk's voice was urgent. "You can do it."

"Is there a way around this?"

"Yes. Cooperation. Doctor McCoy?"

McCoy moved to the viewscreen.

"Admiral, I've isolated the virus and come up with a vaccine. It will do the job if we can get it made and administered fast enough."

"The Romulans were right," added Spock. "The Canara solar system is the nearest and best supply of gran. If the Canarans could be persuaded to let the Romulans purchase their gran, the plague could be averted and peace maintained."

"And just how do you propose to do that? Shall we send the Romulan fleet—which has invaded our space—an engraved invitation to help itself?"

Kirk ignored the sarcasm.

"Let us act as intermediary for the Federation. Commander S'Talon and I will be joint emissaries between Canara and the Romulan empire. What is there to lose?"

"Nothing, I guess. All right, Kirk. You have two solar days. If at the end of that time you cannot come to an agreement, I will have no alternative but to consider this intrusion an act of war and to proceed accordingly."

Poppaelia's voice faded and Kirk took a deep breath.

"Let's get started," he said. "Mister Sulu, warp four."

* * *

The Praetor regarded the elderly man with ill-disguised contempt.

Romm Joramm sat cross-legged on a woven mat, the translucent ivory of his complexion catching the last pale, pink rays of the Canara sun. The single white garment he wore accented the delicacy of his features. Only the knot of gold which clasped the shoulder of his tunic bespoke his rank or wealth. His pale, gold eyes warmed with hospitality.

"So you are the trader Jublius Mannius—please, sit and share the fruits of the land."

He indicated the empty mat with a wave of his hand and the Praetor reluctantly lowered his impressive bulk to the floor.

"You are here to negotiate for our crop—so much you have told my wife. I am sorry to have to refuse, but our treaty with the United Federation of Planets includes the sale of all surplus gran directly to the Federation."

"And if you were to receive the offer of a better price?"

The Praetor's voice was slick with the fat of wealth. He examined the rings on his left hand, judiciously turning it so the jewelry caught the light of the oil lamp and flashed in gaudy splendor.

"Wealth is a very fine thing, but I think there are better. We have received one thing from the Federation that I am not sure you can offer."

"I assure you, elder, we are prepared to pay any price you can name."

"I think you have already forfeited the Federation's price . . . Praetor of the Romulan empire."

"So you have discovered my identity. That is of little consequence. What is this price I cannot match?"

"Why, simple honesty, my Praetor. You have come to me under false pretenses and your story of trading

174

for gran is likely to be a fabrication also. Had you come openly . . . but it is too late to speak of that. Guard, will you escort . . ."

"I think not. You will not touch me or restrict my movements. Even now the Praetorian guard has secured this village and the weapons of the Romulan fleet are trained on the population centers of this planet."

The Praetor spoke with smug authority, but Romm Joramm, elder of Canara, was not visibly impressed.

"That will not help you, lord. Who will harvest the fields if you destroy the people of Canara? In any event, we have taken precautions."

"You?"

The contempt in the Praetor's voice was no longer disguised.

"Yes. You look unconvinced. Jaael."

A young man stepped from the shadows, his slim figure and gold eyes typical of Canara's inhabitants.

"Jaael, please explain to the Praetor the situation as it now stands."

"When we discovered the identity of the visitors we implemented planetary defense . . ."

"I see no defenses. I do not even see weapons. We will take what we want. You must become more adept at deceit if you wish to be believed."

"You speak from experience, no doubt, but wait," replied Romm Joramm.

Jaael continued.

"The incendiaries have been set and at your word they will be ignited. In one minute the fields will be aflame. In one hour there will be nothing left."

"You will destroy yourselves?" The Praetor could not keep the horror from his voice.

"Perhaps. But we will maintain what we are. And we will not have helped our enemies. You see no evidence of warfare? But we are a warrior people. We have spent our lives in constant warfare against our environment. We must fight to survive. And we have learned to prepare ourselves. We are prepared for you."

The Praetor's face was a mask of failure. He was completely at a loss.

"The interview is over." Joramm's voice was suddenly sharp. "You and your fleet will depart Canara or Canara will die. You have six hours, sir!"

Joramm turned his head, shutting the Praetor out as surely as if he had slammed a door in his face. He was insulted and he knew it. That this frail old man could out-maneuver the might of the Romulan empire—he could not accept it. There was a way to defeat this puny, washed-out old fool. He would find it . . . and if he did not, if the empire must die, he would at least have the satisfaction of draining the lifeblood of Canara. He would not kill them—oh, no. But he would scorch their planet until nothing could survive. The water would be tainted and the land sterile. Canara would die in the lingering agony of starvation. Whatever the outcome, they would not win.

"Captain! A message from Star Fleet Command coming in, sir. It's coded and scrambled."

"Put it on the viewer," replied Captain Garson.

"Aye, sir."

Iota winced as Admiral Poppaelia's angular face appeared.

"Captain Garson. Admiral Iota."

Poppaelia's formality made both men uneasy.

"Admiral," acknowledged Garson.

"We have some new information on the Romulan problem. It is more acute than we dreamed. It seems the Romulan empire has, indeed, invaded the boundaries of Federation space . . ."

"What did I tell you? And would you listen? What

are you going to do about it? Or is it already too late?" interrupted Iota accusingly.

"I'm getting to that. It seems we do have a chance for peace. Their purpose is not military."

Poppaelia ignored Iota's explosion, but Garson's look of disbelief unsettled him. If he lost Garson there would be no controlling Iota, and they would be destroyed.

"The Romulans have been attacked by a plague of unbelievable proportions. They desperately need medical assistance."

"Then why didn't they ask for it?" Iota barked.

"Would you have given it to them? That's why. Your reaction speaks for itself. They felt they could expect no help so they decided to try to trade for or take by force the supplies they needed."

"Sir, may I ask the source of this information?" Garson asked.

"Yes. It's a reliable one: Kirk and the *Enterprise*. It seems he managed to capture a Romulan officer who corroborates the story. Moreover, the *Enterprise*'s medical officer has conclusive proof the disease exists. He has come up with a vaccine that can stop the course of the plague—if it can be made and administered fast enough."

"Sir, was there any question as to who was the prisoner of whom? It is completely out of character for a Romulan to allow himself to be captured."

For the first time since they had met, Iota regarded the Potemkin's captain with a tinge of respect.

"No doubt. Not in my mind, at least. As far as I can see Kirk is a free agent. I've given him two solar days to come up with some kind of a solution."

"Don't you think that was a decision for the entire council to make?" said Iota tightly.

"There wasn't time. The Romulan fleet is at Canara. Kirk is taking the *Enterprise* there. He has my authorization to act as intermediary for the Federation, to try to negotiate a settlement. Until that time you will take no action except in self-defense. Justifiable self-defense. Is that clear? You have been apprised of the situation, gentlemen."

Poppaelia's image faded from the screen and the joint commanders looked at one another.

"I don't believe it."

Iota's jaw was set and his voice carried complete conviction.

"I admit it requires a lot of faith, Admiral. But I know Kirk, and his word has always been sounder than most formal treaties."

"I don't doubt your friend, Garson, and I'm aware of his credentials, but who can withstand the kind of brainwashing techniques those savages use? It's all an elaborate plot to take us by surprise. I don't believe it."

"We are under orders, Admiral."

"I can see no valid evidence Kirk is in command of the situation. He could just as easily be a hostage, used to lull us into complacency while the Romulans prepare their attack. I will not sit idly by while the Federation is duped."

"We are under orders," repeated Garson, but the admiral shed his words with a lift of his head.

"I will not stand idly by," he intoned.

Iota was standing behind the command chair in an attitude befitting a conqueror. His head was high, his shoulders squared and there was a light of conviction in his eyes. Garson watched him with growing apprehension and the dawning knowledge he was dealing with a fanatic.

Chapter 13

"Captain's Log: stardate thirty-one twenty-eight point eight, Mikel Garson, Captain, USS *Potemkin*, recording.

"We are holding position at the Neutral Zone awaiting further orders from Star Fleet Command. The situation is intense, nerves are on edge, and I am particularly concerned about Admiral Iota. He seems to be almost pathologically convinced the Romulans intend to provoke a war. I must admit his arguments are not so far-fetched as I first believed, but his obsession with the 'Romulan menace' is frightening. He has been in his quarters since our last contact with Star Fleet Command. I am afraid he is considering some drastic action."

Admiral Iota, Star Fleet Intelligence, member of the Defense Council, known to his friends as 'Jake,' emerged from his quarters. Crewmen, watching him pass, looked twice. The sense of purpose which drew their eyes coursed through his veins like fire. He saw the obvious solution. Only one course promised complete safety for the Federation. So simple. Why hadn't he thought of it before? True, it defied that clacking grandmother Poppaelia's orders, but that was only a technicality. When it was successfully over and he was a hero, the savior of the Federation, no one would remember. Or if they did, it would be to authorize his actions. He smiled as he walked through the last metal doorway separating him from his goal. The doors snapped shut behind him, concealing his presence. A sign on the wall read "Auxiliary Control."

"Captain! My helm control has been cut off! I've lost the ship!"

"Are you sure, Helm? Check that control panel."

Arviela's salt and pepper head bent over the control panel as she checked the circuitry. Her enameled silver nails pressed buttons with deliberate care.

"No, sir. The control panel checks out. Power has been cut off—diverted to some other area."

"Engineering! Are you having difficulties?"

"No, sir, everything's normal down here." The engineer's voice was puzzled.

"Captain . . . I've lost the phasers too—it's like a main power switch has been flipped off."

"Go to manual."

"No manual response, sir."

Garson watched Arviela check the controls for the third time. His worries over Iota became a solid rock in his stomach: he knew what had happened. Iota had sabotaged the manual safeguards, taken over auxiliary control and was at this moment by-passing the main computer.

"Auxiliary control," Garson snapped at the intercom. "Admiral Iota."

"Captain," acknowledged Iota, oozing sarcasm around the title.

"Admiral, I must ask you to return helm and phaser control to the bridge."

"I think not."

"Admiral, I remind you I am military commander of this mission."

"And I will remind you of my rank and my position on the Defense Council. Do you really think Star Fleet Command would, in the end, accept your views over mine?"

"My authority—from the head of the Defense Council—is on record."

"Perhaps, perhaps," Iota answered, "in normal times. But we are at war and war requires drastic measures. If we sit here and wait for the Romulans to shoot first we're throwing away the best chance we have!"

"Admiral, no one has made a move! The Romulans are completely within their rights! You can't fire on them!"

"The Romulan fleet has invaded Federation space."

Iota's voice stated this fact as if it were a religious tenet repeated in blind faith. Garson was helpless to combat his righteous conviction. Physical battles he could fight, diplomatic discussions he could cope with, but he had no idea how to pierce Iota's blindness.

"Admiral, wait! Please give it some time. You can always attack. Just give me some time!"

"There is no time."

"Yes, there is! One day! Just one day and I'll give in."

Garson caught a flicker of hesitation on the admiral's face and pressed harder.

"Do it for the Federation you love. Give peace a chance before you plunge into war. Please, Admiral, think of the Federation."

"I think only of the Federation. All right, Captain, one day. But that is all. If at the end of that time peace has not been declared, this ship will attack the enemy. One day," repeated the admiral as he switched off the intercom.

Captain Garson drew a deep breath and let it out slowly. One day. He had no ship, no weapons. At least the other ships were functional . . . and he still had communications. He had told Iota relying on Kirk was a matter of faith. The truth of his own statement mocked him.

"Lieutenant, get me Poppaelia. Block the transmission so it can't be monitored by Auxiliary Control."

"Aye, sir. I have him, sir."

"On the screen."

"Yes, Garson?"

Poppaelia sounded annoyed and Garson could not blame him.

"I am afraid I'm forced to add to your burdens, sir. I must report that Admiral Iota has barricaded himself in Auxiliary Control and now holds weaponry, helm and navigational systems. He refuses to believe the Romulans do not want war. He has issued an ultimatum: if he does not have conclusive proof peace is declared within twenty-four hours, he will attack the Romulan ships in the Neutral Zone."

"My God!"

Garson nodded.

"I'll do my best to outmaneuver him, sir, but there's only one sure way I can see to stop him."

"Don't do it until the last moment. Keep at him. I know he's a fanatic, but I don't think he's completely crazy. I think you can still get through to him."

"Sir, he has very little respect for me."

Poppaelia snorted.

"He has little respect for anyone, but he's big on facts. Do your best. If Kirk comes through . . ."

Poppaelia left the sentence unfinished as his image faded from the screen. Kirk was the fulcrum of the situation. If he could push things the Federation's way—and he had managed some tight spots before—there might be a chance to defeat the admiral's obsession. Garson clung to this isolated sliver of hope.

"Captain, I have Canara on the sensors. ETA, forty minutes."

"Very good, Mister Spock. Mister Chekov, put us in standard orbit around Canara, but keep the Romulan fleet on the other side of the planet at all times."

"That will require an oblique approach, Captain," replied the navigator. "It will take longer."

"Yes. I don't want the Romulans to know we're here . . . yet."

"Aye, sir."

Spock turned from the computer station and went quietly to the captain's side. Kirk looked up from the report he had just signed. His eyes held an unspoken question.

"I have investigated the Canarans, Captain. They are indeed a primal and ruthless people, but they are endeavoring to extend their knowledge. The head of the Canaran council of elders, Romm Joramm, is in a large measure responsible for this. I believe if he can be convinced to deal with the Romulans there is hope bloodshed may be avoided."

"This . . . Romm Joramm . . . how does he feel about the Federation?"

"It was through his leadership Canara became a member of the Federation."

"Then we should be able to come to some agreement."

"Yes . . . but it would be unwise to discount the stubbornness and severity of the Canaran people. Once committed to a line of action, they are not easily swayed."

Uhura cupped a hand over the subspace receiver in her ear. She cocked her head to catch a faint signal.

"Sir, I'm picking up a distress signal from Canara. It's faint, sir. They're requesting assistance from Star Fleet."

"Good. They should welcome us, then."

"Fortuitous indeed, Captain," commented Spock.

"Jim, timely though our arrival may be, how do you think the Canarans will react when they find there are Romulans aboard the *Enterprise?*" asked Doctor McCoy.

"That does present a problem," murmured Kirk with a glance at S'Talon.

"Indeed, Captain. The Canarans may believe they are being manipulated. And if you present me as a prisoner of war they are not likely to accept me as an ambassador," interposed S'Talon.

"Mmmm . . . Lieutenant Uhura, open a channel to Canara—scrambled—I want to speak with Romm Joramm."

"Aye, sir."

"Perhaps, Captain, it would be better if I withdrew during your interview," said S'Talon.

"Thank you, Commander. That would be wise. Doctor McCoy, would you escort the commander?"

"I'd be happy to. Sir?"

The Romulan leveled a look at Kirk, a warning against betrayal. He watched the human's changing hazel eyes absorb the warning and respond. "Trust me," they said. He had no alternative . . . trust was

184

the only chance the empire had. For himself, he was lost. He knew when he looked on the Praetor's face he would see his own death.

"I have Romm Joramm, sir."

Kirk waited until S'Talon and McCoy had left before he replied.

"Put him on the screen, Lieutenant."

"Aye, sir," acknowledged Uhura.

Kirk had never met a Canaran. Except for the vaguest generalizations and the information Spock had given him, he knew nothing about Canara, but Romm Joramm impressed him. The man's immense dignity gave his frail body stature. It flowed through his movements and hung in the drapery of his clothing. His pale gold eyes were translucent.

"Welcome," he said. "I am Romm Joramm, leader of the Council of Elders."

"James Kirk, sir, commanding the USS *Enterprise*. We heard your distress signal."

"Yes. We are in most dire need of help. We have been invaded by Romulans. They came disguised as traders, demanding gran. When we refused they said they would take what they needed. We told them we would destroy the crop. In turn, I think they will destroy us."

"Sir, would you consider letting the Romulans buy your gran—at a fair price?"

Kirk's face held all the earnest honesty of a cherub.

"If they had come to us openly . . . but no. They have lied; they must take the consequences. But why do you ask—are you with them? Is this a trick?"

The old man's voice sharpened suddenly and Kirk thanked the providence that had removed S'Talon from the bridge. It had been a wise move.

"No. No. But there are extenuating circumstances."

Romm Joramm checked his rising anger and waited for an explanation. The captain launched his argument.

"The Romulan empire is, itself, under attack—not by military force, but by disease. A plague has destroyed one-third of the population. There is a medicine that can stop the plague, but to make it they need gran. Their own supplies ran out long ago. They come to you wounded and for that reason they are dangerous, for they have nothing to lose. If you will sell them gran there is a chance the Romulan empire will survive and you will prevent a galactic war."

"The Romulans are enemies of the Federation. Why do we not simply allow them to die? The life of this planet would not be too high a price to pay for the survival of the whole Federation, unmolested by this outside menace."

"Sir, I will be honest with you. There are many who see no objection to what you propose. It would seem to be a practical solution. But it means war. And war means suffering and death for both sides. It is in our best interest to prevent it."

Joramm considered this.

"I see," he said. Suddenly he smiled. "It means we must place what we would like to do behind the welfare of the people. That is a lesson, Captain, I have been working on all my life. I doubt that I shall ever master it. However, in this instance, I see in the bending of my will a measure of profit. Not only will Canara survive, it will become rich—at least by our standards."

The captain felt relief flow through his body. He answered Joramm's smile with his own. "Thank you, sir," he said.

"Thank you, young man. I owe you a debt for curbing my temper. You are," he added with a twinkle, "extremely persuasive."

"I have a temper of my own, sir," replied Kirk, "and it has often been diverted by the hand of a friend."

S'Talon fingered the plump leaf of a violet, touched the delicate blue and white blossom. McCoy busied himself picking the dead blooms from a small magnolia tree. He kept an eye on the Romulan, but did not intrude upon his privacy. The botany lab was fresh with the smell of growing things. If there were only a breeze the doctor could have shut his eyes and pretended he was home in Georgia.

"What a lush place your Earth must be, Doctor, to be so filled with beauty."

The still air quelled S'Talon's voice and the deep quiet of the plants swallowed it, but McCoy still heard his murmured comment.

"Yes, it is," he answered.

S'Talon looked up sharply. Dark Romulan eyes under angled brows scanned the Terran's face. It was crossed with a pain he did not understand. "Is there something wrong, Doctor? You look as if you do not feel well."

"I don't," said McCoy.

"Then help must be summoned. Your sickbay . . ."

"No, Commander, I'm not ill."

McCoy paused, uncertain what to say.

"There is pain in your eyes—surely not without cause."

"The centurion, Commander. I am so sorry. If only we had discovered the vaccine in time she might still be alive."

S'Talon's mind clouded. He would feel S'Tarleya's loss for the rest of his life, but it had not been anyone's fault. If guilt existed, it was his, for blindness. He turned, his deep eyes seeking the doctor's.

"It could not be helped, Doctor. S'Tarleya was

187

pleased there was a chance for the rest of her people. She said you told her she was the instrument of their survival." These humans were the strangest combination of strength and weakness. "Is there hope, Doctor? Can your captain produce miracles?"

McCoy smiled.

"Some think he can, Commander. He will do his best . . . and that is exceptional."

"Of that, Doctor, I have ample proof," replied S'Talon.

"He's one of a kind," said McCoy.

"Let us hope so," said S'Talon so fervently the doctor chuckled.

The intercom sounded and McCoy dug behind a large philodendron and activated it.

"McCoy here."

"Kirk here. Bones, the Canarans have agreed to sell their gran to the Romulans and they've accepted S'Talon as the Romulan ambassador. Please have S'Talon return to Control. It's time to hood the falcon."

"That may not be easy, Captain."

Kirk swiveled the command chair to face his first officer.

"You're telling me," he murmured. "We've got to place them at a disadvantage."

"We do have them at a technical disadvantage. They have invaded our territory and threatened aggression against a member of the Federation. The practical situation is, however, entirely different," said Spock.

"One ship against the entire Romulan fleet." Kirk bent his head. "One ship," he murmured reflectively. "Our only chance is to surprise them—command the situation intellectually."

"Canara coming up, sir," interposed Sulu.

"Standard orbit, Mister Sulu."

"Aye, Captain. Standard orbit."

"Captain, the Romulan fleet is on the other side of the planet," said Chekov.

The captain ran a finger across his lower lip.

"Mister Chekov, plot an intercept course that will put us right in the middle of them. No shields. Stand by. Doctor McCoy to Control," he said to Uhura.

Chekov and Sulu exchanged glances. Chekov took a deep breath and carried out the captain's order.

"Course plotted, sir," he said.

"Warp one, Mister Sulu."

"Aye, sir."

The *Enterprise* sailed into the heart of the Romulan fleet with the aplomb of an ancient wooden vessel under full sail. She glided gracefully to a halt in front of the Praetor's flagship. Like the proverbial fair and innocent maiden, she floated serenely in the midst of a pack of hungry wolves.

"The man is mad!"

"Not mad, my Praetor, but very, very clever," said a Romulan officer. "That is the *Enterprise,* commanded by Kirk. I have faced him before. He never does anything without a reason."

The Praetor glared at the Federation starship.

"This is how S'Talon buys time!" he said, contempt in his voice. "I will talk with this Kirk! Open a communications channel."

"At once, Praetor."

Stars melted from the Romulan viewscreen and alien faces took their places . . . alien except for one.

"S'Talon!" snarled the Praetor. "This is what you have done for the empire!"

He spat the words and S'Talon straightened imperceptibly.

"Yes, my Praetor," he answered steadily.

The Praetor! Kirk and his bridge crew studied the Romulan leader with undisguised curiosity. They saw a huge man whose handsome features were stained with pride, passion and ruthless self-interest. Kirk knew immediately this man would do nothing for the sake of the empire that did not also directly benefit himself.

"Where is your ship, S'Talon? And your crew?" said the Praetor in a soft voice with razor-sharp edges.

"His ship is destroyed and his crew are dead or aboard this vessel."

"Kirk," guessed the Praetor.

"Sir," he acknowledged.

"So. You have S'Talon and his crew . . . and I have you. An entertaining situation."

"More than entertaining, sir: cataclysmic. If you choose to make it so."

"I, Captain? I hardly think you are in a position to be belligerent."

"No," said Kirk, challenge slashing from his eyes, "I have come to plead with you! For our lives . . . and the life of the Romulan empire."

"The Romulan empire is not your concern, Captain."

"You have invaded Federation space—that makes it my concern. Your people are dying. Unless you receive immediate help, there will be no empire, only a handful of scattered survivors. Hardly fit to rule," he added deviously.

"We can do very well without you, Captain."

"No. You have already found out the Canarans are loyal to the Federation. Without the sanction of the Federation they will never give you the gran you need. And you will not be able to take it. If you attempt force they will destroy the entire supply. You need me, Praetor."

"I am to trust to the Federation's good will to supply medical assistance to its enemies?"

"You must. And good will is hardly our motive. Canara is a member of the Federation and as such deserves Federation protection and assistance—we can hardly allow you to pillage as you please. By your blatant military entry into Federation space you have jeopardized the fragile truce we maintain. We do not desire war. The cost to both sides would be astronomical. And Canara is the nearest major source of gran. By the time you found another supply, it would be too late to matter."

"What you say has the uncomfortable feel of truth," murmured the Praetor.

"An empire of the dead is no empire," said Kirk. "I have always been impressed by the military calibre of Romulan warriors. You are fortunate, sir, to have officers of Commander S'Talon's quality. His foresight may well save the situation. Surely the Emperor will repay the one who is responsible for the very existence of the Romulan race. Such a man would be honored everywhere . . . the . . . rewards . . . would be incalculable."

Kirk watched the Praetor sniff at the bait. Fame—and fortune—have a pleasant scent, and the Romulan was on the verge of intoxication when he pulled his desires to a halt.

"The welfare of the people is my first concern," he stated pompously.

"Of course, sir," answered Kirk, suppressing a smile.

"If you will beam S'Talon aboard, we can proceed with the negotiations."

"I think not. The Commander has knowledge valuable to our medical staff . . ."

"That's right," said McCoy. "We've isolated the mutation in the virus and are making extensive tests to determine the effectiveness of a vaccine."

"Besides," added Kirk, "the Commander is much too valuable as an intermediary. The Canarans have agreed to accept S'Talon as the Romulan envoy."

The Praetor looked down his long and elegant nose. So. S'Talon could not be made a scapegoat. Well, he would claim S'Talon's glory—so he got only enough to save his life. That was more than he deserved. He allowed the silence to lengthen. His voice, when he spoke, was superior and a little bored.

"We will allow this," he said royally.

Kirk smiled.

"Good. Negotiations will begin immediately. The commander will inform you of the details."

Kirk stepped back to allow S'Talon exclusive use of the communications line.

"You would seem to have averted disaster, Captain."

Spock was at his elbow.

"Keep your fingers crossed," answered the captain.

Spock tilted his head, considering.

"What possible effect can crossing the fingers produce? I was not aware of any extraordinary human abilities . . ."

Kirk chuckled, tension draining away.

"Only you, Spock," said McCoy.

Chapter 14

S'Tokkr, science officer of the Romulan ship *Eagle,* rubbed his forehead with the back of his hand. He knew he was ill, but he had no time for infirmities of the flesh. Without his expertise the bridge crew would be crippled. The vessel was badly understaffed—more so even than those which followed the Praetor. At this moment he manned both his own science station and the special weapons console.

S'Tokkr shook his head to clear it and sent a wave of dizziness over his mind. His close-fitting helmet was stifling. He felt squeezed inside it, unable to breathe. In desperation, regulations or no regulations, he wrenched it off. Breathing deeply, he forced his eyes back to the scanners, determined to remain at his post. He blinked hard, willing his eyes to focus on the screens. The fluctuating computer patterns held him mesmerized and he knew he was fighting a losing battle. He opened his mouth to summon help, but no sound came. His eyes rolled up and he collapsed on the console.

"Captain!"

An engineering technician pointed to S'Tokkr's supine form.

The Romulan captain growled an oath.

"Remove him!"

S'Tokkr's body was dragged from its post with little delicacy. His lifeless hands rattled keys as they slid across the console. One finger knocked against a small, orange lever hard enough to move it. No one noticed.

"Captain, the cloaking device!"

Arviela's exclamation knocked Garson out of his reverie. His eyes snapped to the viewscreen just in time to see the last of the Romulan ships wink out of sight.

"Ship's status?"

"Our shields have been activated."

"Get me an open channel to the rest of the fleet!"

"Our course is being charted into the Neutral Zone!" interposed the navigator.

"You're on, sir."

"This is Garson of the *Potemkin*. You all know how the situation stands. No vessel in this detachment will enter the Neutral Zone without my express order." There was a painful pause. It took an immense effort of will for Garson to issue his next order. "Should the *Potemkin* begin to move toward the Neutral Zone, all ships will block her path. If this does not deter her, you are authorized to shoot her down. Stop her any way you can."

Garson indicated the end of the transmission with a wave of his hand and then said, "Get me Iota."

Iota sat hunched in his chair, oblivious of the captain's summons. He concentrated on the course he was plotting toward the last position of the Romulan vessels.

"Give it up, Admiral!"

Garson's voice held a note of command Iota had not previously heard.

"They've activated the cloaking device. It's clear they mean to attack! I'm going to be there first!"

Iota punched a button and Arviela murmured, "Half impulse power."

"This time I hold the high card, Admiral," said Garson.

Iota's arrogance turned to shocked disbelief as the rest of the Federation detachment glided into the *Potemkin*'s path. His sensors told him their defense shields were in place.

"Checkmate, Admiral."

"What is the meaning of this?"

"If you attempt to take the *Potemkin* into the Neutral Zone, the rest of the fleet will destroy us."

"The Romulans attack!"

"We will not."

"You're bluffing."

"Try me."

Garson's voice was chilling in its certainty.

Iota hesitated, then touched another control and the ship hung in space.

"I did, after all, give you twenty-four hours. Eight remain. After that I will not hesitate to use the facilities at my disposal. This discussion is terminated."

The screen went dark. Garson rose from his command chair and began a meandering tour of the bridge. His frown cut a V of wrinkles on his usually untroubled forehead as he wrestled with an impossible impasse.

"What!"

Tiercellus leaped to his feet with the agility of a

twenty-year-old acrobat and immediately regretted it, but he was too preoccupied to worry about the stitch in his side.

"As I stated, sir, the *Eagle*'s cloaking device was inadvertently activated. Because the *Eagle* was your ship, the other vessels assumed they were to follow suit. We estimate the fleet has been invisible for a quarter," answered the *Eagle*'s captain.

"And the Federation vessels?"

"One started to move toward the Neutral Zone, but the others cut her off. They were running with full shields."

"Most unusual. Deactivate the device, Captain, and signal the other ships as well. The time has not yet come to engage the enemy. We are the Praetor's insurance. We must never forget that fact and be ready to aid him should he need us."

"I obey."

Tiercellus struggled into his tunic, favoring his right side. He removed a bottle, vial and glass from a storage cabinet and poured himself a healthy dose of blue ale. Its power would cover the unpleasant taste of his medication. He carefully squeezed three drops of blood-red liquid into the ale, lifted the glass and stirred the mixture with a circular motion of his hand. It was a deep purple draught, rich as the border on the Emperor's robe, royal as the heritage of the Romulan way. He drank it in one swallow and made his way toward the bridge.

His movements were more sure, more decisive than they had been. There was a spring in his step the years had ground away. He would not survive this encounter. He had accepted his fate. Still, he would choose his own good time to die.

As he entered the ship's bridge, the *Eagle*'s captain vacated his position with obsequious haste. Once Tiercellus would have refused this courtesy, but not now. He sank into the comfort of the command chair with a grateful nod to the captain.

"Call weapons master Hexce to the bridge," he said to the communications engineer. "And I would speak with the *Potemkin*'s captain. We will try to decipher his reasons for attacking his own fleet."

Hexce, in response to Tiercellus' call, appeared on the bridge. One glance told him his commander's condition. He moved unobtrusively to a position just behind the command chair.

"Federation starship *Potemkin*. Supreme Commander of the Fleet Tiercellus will speak with your captain! Reply!"

The Romulan's command was answered almost instantly.

"Well, Tiercellus. So you decided to show yourself."

The human's insinuation of cowardice left the Romulan unruffled.

"Were I you, Captain," he countered, "I would speak more diplomatically to a superior adversary."

"I see no evidence of superiority, sir. Merely a certain flair for deceit and trickery."

"I, at least, have control of my forces."

"And I do not?" queried Garson. The bluff he was running was enormous.

"Is it a normal procedure for one Federation ship to attack another? I have always considered mutiny outside accepted regulations. Perhaps this is a Romulan prejudice."

Garson gave a short, wicked chuckle.

"It got you back out in the open, didn't it?"

"Your actions in no way determine mine," returned Tiercellus.

Garson's chuckle sounded again.

"I suggest, sir, you and your fleet retire—this time in actual fact—from the area. Your presence here is a waste of time for both of us."

"That may be, Captain, but the Romulan empire does not act out of expediency to the Federation. You will yield, sir—now—or later, in a much less . . ." he paused, amusement in his eyes ". . . humane manner. The choice is yours, sir."

Tiercellus severed communications and sank back in the command chair. He tried to relax, but Hexce could see the rapid pulse in the prominent blood vessels of his old commander's hands.

"You will be needed, Hexce, and soon," said Tiercellus softly.

Garson let his breath escape between his teeth in a relieved whistle.

"Close call, sir."

Arviela's comment produced a nod from Garson.

"Too close. We've got to get that crackpot out of auxiliary control."

"I've gone over every single thing I can think of to pry him out of there, and drawn a blank. He could barricade himself forever. Nothing's going to touch him short of destruction of the ship," said the *Potemkin*'s science officer.

"Can't we flood the compartment with tranquilizer gas—something?"

"Not without his knowing it. That's the real problem, sir. Anything we do down there can be detected."

Garson considered the risk and found it too great. No matter what they used, Iota would be able to take some action before he lost consciousness, and that action might provoke war. Deep in his heart, Garson knew he would sacrifice the *Potemkin* and its crew to prevent that.

"Then all we have is the human factor."

Garson's voice held little confidence. Trying to reach the shreds of sanity lurking in the twisted corridors of Iota's mind was going to be difficult. He did not consider an understanding of complex personal relationships to be his forte. Sane, Iota was an insular personality; mad, he was a depth charge waiting for detonation. He might already be irrevocably primed for disaster. Yet Poppaelia seemed to feel there was a chance to get through to him.

"There's one thing, sir," said Arviela.

"Yes, Lieutenant?"

"He doesn't want to die. He backed off when the rest of the fleet confronted him. Maybe if he had a good excuse to give in . . ."

"I see your point."

"Message coming in, sir. It's Admiral Poppaelia," interposed Commander Yellowhorse at the communications post.

"On screen."

Poppaelia's leathery face was positively wreathed in smiles and Garson's heart lifted for the first time in hours. Poppaelia launched his news with no preliminary.

"Garson, we've heard from Kirk! He's arranged a truce whereby the Federation and the Romulan empire can resolve their differences. No war. That should get you off the hook."

"Good news, Admiral. Very good news, indeed. What about the situation here?"

"What you're facing there, Garson, is the Romulan rear guard."

"I don't suppose the truce will affect their position."

"Hardly."

"Couldn't you ask them to withdraw?"

"We've tried that. They won't budge. The Praetor was adamant. And since they, at least, are not in violation of treaty, there isn't much we can do."

"I understand, Admiral."

"Quit worrying, Garson. We've averted war."

"Maybe," muttered Garson to himself. Aloud he said, "I'll consolidate matters here. Except for our . . . personal difficulties . . . things are static."

"Satisfactory. Let me know if you need help. Report any changes in the situation immediately. Poppaelia out."

Garson nodded to Yellowhorse.

"Admiral Iota, sir."

"Good news, Admiral." Garson tried to channel every ounce of confidence he could muster into his voice. "The Romulan crisis has been resolved. Peace is declared."

"I heard."

"Then you know there's no longer any reason for aggression against the Romulans."

"I know nothing of the kind. I see four Romulan ships. They have not withdrawn. There is no peace."

"Surely you don't disbelieve Admiral Poppaelia?"

"Bah. That bleeding-heart? He'd lie through his teeth to avoid honest combat. As a matter of fact, he did lie."

"What do you mean, Admiral?"

"Quit while you're ahead, Garson. You know as well as I Kirk is dead. I'm surprised at you Garson. I'm not that easily duped."

Garson spoke slowly, trying to pound each word into Iota's armored mind.

"James Kirk is not dead. He has negotiated peace between the Federation and the Romulan empire. There is no reason for hostility."

"Don't make me laugh. You won't fool me with childish tricks. And you will not deprive me of the rewards of my actions. You now have two hours in which to negotiate. I suggest you make use of them. Iota out."

Garson slumped heavily against the front of the helm console. Somewhere there had to be a key to unlock Iota's mind. The man's confidence in his own judgment had to be shaken, shaken so hard its back was broken. It was clear he required proof of any statement, no matter what its source. Garson acknowledged himself a fool for not realizing this earlier. He had actually expected the news of Kirk's success to change Iota's position. Well, it had not. No hearsay would ever do that. Iota had to hear things for himself or he did not believe them. As an intelligence expert he would be inundated with false and conflicting opinions, would learn to trust nothing but hard fact. Garson felt he had played his last card. The destruction of the *Potemkin* was beginning to look inescapable.

S'Talon surveyed the comfortable but sterile quarters he occupied with a dissatisfaction verging on anger. He had no justification for his feelings as far as his treatment was concerned. He had met with respect and courtesy on every hand.

True, he and his crew were still virtual prisoners of the Federation, but he had to admit it was as much for his protection as a lever against the empire. Security guards were his constant companions, but he was used to that.

He looked around his apartment again. It had all the necessities but not one element of personality. The room was barren except for a long-range, sub-space communicator, pre-set and locked on the Praetor's frequency, and a portable viewer accompanied by a collection of tapes, kindly lent him by Spock. Yet it felt like home. That was it! That was what was making him so disagreeable.

S'Talon isolated his reaction and studied it. This lifeless atmosphere, untouched by the core of his personality, felt comfortable. Had he lived in such anonymity always? Was it of his own making? He did not know. He only knew he was now aware of it. S'Tarleya's love, however brief his knowledge of it, had awakened him to the singleminded narrowness of his own life. He found, after all, that his career could not contain him. For the first time in his life his sense of purpose was an inadequate defense against loneliness.

"I see I am intruding, Commander."

The *Enterprise*'s Vulcan first officer stood in the doorway, his hands cradling something. S'Talon was startled, but glad of the interruption. His thoughts led to a dark door closed to his perception.

"On the contrary, I welcome your company. I find my own thoughts disquieting."

"That is unfortunate, since they must be your inseparable comrades."

"My ill temper robs me of manners. My thanks for your thoughtfulness," said S'Talon, indicating the pile of tapes.

"I am well aware of the effects of boredom. It is a disorder particularly devastating to humans."

"They are an unpredictable lot, if your captain and medical officer are representative."

"They are a continual source of interest," agreed Spock. "However, a discussion of Captain Kirk is not my motive for seeking you out."

S'Talon almost smiled at Spock's rebuke and his own incorrigible desire to amass information on a formidable opponent.

"What, then, is your errand? I had thought agreement had been reached between my people and yours."

"I am not here in my capacity as a Star Fleet officer, but as a distant kinsman."

With these words he placed a handsome carving on the table before S'Talon. The stylized bird of prey had a profound effect on the Romulan. Spock watched S'Talon's eyes turn to pools of bottomless black and noted the uncontrolled grief they expressed.

"It was found among the centurion's personal belongings. Doctor McCoy said she requested it be given to you, Commander."

A short flash of anger for the alien's intrusion on S'Tarleya's privacy hit S'Talon before he acknowledged the necessity of searching a prisoner's belongings. He knew he would have been less generous, would have confiscated all personal possessions. No doubt the t'liss had been thoroughly checked as a possible instrument of sabotage or escape. That S'Tarleya had managed to salvage the one item he cherished touched the Romulan deeply. It was a fitting gift from her, encompassing as it did the austere ideal of the warrior.

Spock ran a sensitive finger over the satiny wood with an appreciation S'Talon had not expected.

"It is a thing of beauty, Commander."

"Yes. And of a rarity I had not before realized."

The Romulan spoke of something far more valuable than a work of art and Spock found himself regretting the political and ideological barriers between them. Yet for a few short hours Romulan, Vulcan and human had managed to accept their differences and combine their energies to prevent a war and shackle disease. Perhaps it was a beginning.

The Romulan communications officer whirled in his chair, his eyes incredulous.

"Sir! A message from the Praetor! They have declared . . . peace!"

Tiercellus straightened with an effort and leaned forward.

"Details," he commanded.

"His most glorious excellency . . ."

Tiercellus grimaced.

". . . has declared peace between the Romulan empire and the United Federation of Planets . . . we have obtained sufficient supplies to stem the plague."

"It seems we are not to die in battle after all, my friend," said Tiercellus.

Hexce smiled.

"We are cheated even of that," he agreed.

"Our orders are to make no move, but to maintain our position here on the borders of the Neutral Zone. The Praetor's fleet will rendezvous with us when they have completed negotiations."

Tiercellus sank into his chair. He was drained of purpose, yet Hexce could see the command the old man exercised over his body. Wracked with pain, he was using the last of his mental strength to subdue it.

"The crisis passes, Hexce, and so must I," said Tiercellus softly. His hands were braced against the arms of his chair and his breath now came in short, harsh gasps.

"No."

Hexce's voice, low and broken, surprised Tiercellus. Their comradeship went deeper than he had realized. The sorrow, the protest in the big engineer's voice warmed Tiercellus even as he felt the cold cloak of death begin to close around his body.

"Remember your promise, Hexce."

Hexce nodded.

"I will keep my oath to the death," he replied.

Tiercellus raised one hand and grasped Hexce's massive forearm in salute.

"We will meet again, Hexce, in that isle reserved for all old comrades and respected enemies. I shall await you, my steadfast friend," Tiercellus whispered.

They were his last words.

So the eagle of the Romulan empire died.

Hexce felt his commander's grip loosen. His face set

in a granite mask of sorrow, but he rose to the task Tiercellus had set him. He got slowly to his feet. The bridge was still. Hexce's eyes swept captain and crew. They were stunned, suddenly weak.

"I thought he would live forever," murmured the captain.

Hexce, aware of the void in his own heart, was quick to recognize it in another's. Tiercellus had been right. He was needed.

"Captain, if you will check the sealed order tapes, you will see I am now in command of the detachment. I know my appointment is somewhat irregular, but you will find it is in total accord with Supreme Commander Tiercellus' authorization. His body is to be prepared for burial and treated with all the respect it is due."

The captain punched up the orders and Hexce watched as Tiercellus' body was borne away. His piercing eyes sparked as he noted the careless indifference of one of the orderlies, and he vowed to teach the man respect for the dead. The methods he contemplated were not gentle.

The Romulan captain turned from the computer tape and saluted Hexce. Though the form of his action was correct, it was clear he did not relish being commanded by an engineer who, until a few moments past, was his distinct inferior in the chain of command. It was also clear Tiercellus' orders were not to be countermanded or disputed. Hexce ignored the captain's arrogance. Like his old commander, he had little to lose.

"Well, Captain, our orders are plain. We await the Praetor. In the meantime, I shall be in engineering. My supervision is required." Hexce paused, sure the captain was not listening to him. His voice became a whip, lashing out with deadly accuracy. "Remember, Captain, we are under a truce. Though he wished for death in battle, Tiercellus knew his own desires were of small importance next to the preservation of the empire. He will be your example . . . you will await my command."

The captain's inattention vanished.

"I hear and obey," he answered. There was a sincerity in his voice which caused Hexce a private smile. He was not without a temper, and the captain knew it.

Chapter 15

Admiral Iota surveyed the slick efficiency of Auxiliary Control with the pride of ownership. He allowed himself to enjoy the compact power at his fingertips. Everything was so carefully designed it created the illusion a single man could handle the ship. Mentally he checked off vital ship's stations: communications, helm, navigation, engineering, a mini science-computer center . . . weapons.

Weapons. They were the ship's real power—not her warp speed engines, but the ability to destroy the enemy. Between phasers and photon torpedoes the *Potemkin*'s destructive potential was considerable. Not much could stand against her. Iota ran his hand over the phaser control panel, thinking of past conquests and the long line of heroic tradition. He belonged to that tradition. Men like Garson and Kirk never realized that. They always believed they held active commands due to some temperamental superiority. What was it Poppaelia had said? That his talent had always been for "internal affairs." He'd show him. He'd show them all. The great gods of Star Fleet were blind to the Romulan menace. No doubt they would still be sitting in their chairs when headquarters itself was destroyed. He would not. He was about to show them who the real man of action was. The thought gave Iota a small curl of pleasure.

He crouched over the weapons station, his eyes on the timer before him. One finger was poised above the photon torpedoes, directly over a button marked "fire." In moments the day of grace he had awarded Garson would end. Iota's eyes never wavered from the timer as he silently counted off the seconds. His excitement mounted as they clicked away.

"Five, four, three, two, one!" he mouthed and his eyes ignited as he pushed the button.

The dim lighting in the captain's cabin was meant to simulate night. It painted the walls with dark, velvety shadows and spread a transparent wash of peace over the room. A grill-work partition cast its geometric pattern across the bed where James Kirk was stretched out. He was catching up on some much-needed rest. His hands were linked across his stomach and one leg was cocked. Every inch of his compact, muscular frame reflected tranquility. His eyes were closed and his breathing deep, but he was not asleep. His senses were acutely active. In this deeper state of mental rest which comes from concentrated relaxation he found a green oasis devoid of responsibility.

He was aware of sound. The ship roared around him, its gentle vibration magnified by his receptivity. It throbbed through bone and muscle, its pulse his. He thought fleetingly of the computer's statement he and the ship were joined, and had to admit in some ways it was right, though the joining was on a different level . . . more his love of an idea.

Thoughts wandered through his mind like a child through a garden, swayed by any fancy. He turned them over in idle curiosity and wondered at them, but the sharp perception of his conscious mind was subdued. Like a timeless summer afternoon, it was full of sun-washed indolence. He reached out for its warm expanse of peace, found it and sank into it.

"Captain Kirk."

His name touched the fringes of his thoughts and he was immediately alert. His eyes snapped open and with one fluid move he rolled to his feet and reached for the intercom.

"Kirk here."

"Captain, I have a message from Admiral Poppaelia," said Uhura. "He requests you take it on the bridge, sir."

"I'm on my way."

An icy tingle ran across the captain's shoulder blades. He shrugged it off. What could possibly happen now, with peaceful negotiations underway and everybody's best interest served?

"Bridge," he told the turbo-lift.

His mind accelerated with his ascent. When he stepped onto the bridge he found it undisturbed, but Lieutenant Uhura's eyes were worried. Kirk nodded to her.

"Put him on, Lieutenant."

"Aye, sir."

"Admiral."

"I am the tale-bearer of disaster, Captain. The *Potemkin* has fired on the Romulan cortege on the borders of the Neutral Zone."

"What?!!"

"Your hearing is not faulty, Captain."

"What did Garson think he was doing? Was he provoked?"

"Captain Garson was not at fault. Admiral Iota has seized auxiliary control and opened fire on the enemy. Your situation is most grave. Withdrawal at the earliest opportunity is advisable."

"Admiral, why hasn't the Romulan fleet exploded? They've made no move at all."

"So far none of the shots have landed. Garson contacted the other vessels in the detachment and they've been shielding the Romulans and countering Iota's fire. So far it's worked, but it's a risky business and sooner or later one of those shots will get through. Iota's fired only the photon torpedoes—if he uses the phasers it'll be almost impossible to stop him."

"Captain, Captain Garson is calling, sir. He says it's urgent."

Kirk half-turned toward his communications officer and Poppaelia noticed the distraction.

"Face it, Jim. Quit trying to find alternatives. Get out of there while you still can!" he said.

"Captain, eight Romulan vessels have moved into position around us," interposed Sulu. "We're surrounded."

"That tears it! Admiral, it seems the Romulan fleet is warned. We will find a way out of this or . . ." He left the sentence unfinished.

"Good luck, Captain," said Poppaelia gently. The viewscreen flickered and the admiral was gone.

"Put Garson on."

"Aye, sir," answered Uhura.

"Jim!"

"Yes, Mikel. Is there any way out of this mess?"

"I don't know. Maybe. So far none of his shots have hit and the Romulans haven't reacted at all. Remarkable forbearance on their part. I've come near ordering the destruction of the ship. I've given Iota one hour to surrender auxiliary control—if he doesn't I'll have no alternative. I don't have much hope . . . he's never trusted me. I thought if you talked to him—from the heart of things—maybe he'd listen."

"You think I can reach him?"

"I don't know. He is completely obsessed by the idea of the Romulans as enemies. He refuses to believe we've made a peaceful settlement with them. He thinks we're all fools."

"Who would he believe?"

"His own people? He's never mentioned allegiance to anything but 'the Federation'—no mention of friends or family."

"Doesn't he have something to do with intelligence and counter-espionage?"

"Yes."

"He talks like it," muttered Yellowhorse.

"Admiral Iota is the nominal director of the Federation Intelligence Corps," said Spock. "He has been instrumental in the development of countless intelligence devices."

Kirk's eyes lit up.

"Like that sensor unit!"

"Precisely, Captain."

"Listen, Garson, there may be a way. Do you know if Iota is in touch with his people?"

"He does have a special wrist communicator . . . I've never seen him without it."

"Then I think we may have an outside chance. Lieutenant Uhura, get S'Talon. Spock, activate that sensor unit . . . and let's make sure any mental images it picks up are related to peaceful cooperation."

"Affirmative, Captain."

Spock reached over to the corner of his computer station and slid his fingers across its surface. A high-pitched whir, audible only to Vulcan ears mentally attuned to it, was the sole evidence of the sensor's activation. Spock looked up and nodded.

"Good!" Kirk took a deep breath. "Have you got S'Talon, Lieutenant?"

"Not yet, sir. I . . . here he is, Captain."

"Commander S'Talon," greeted Kirk.

"Captain, what is the meaning of this? I have just received word a Federation vessel has opened fire on four of our ships! I thought we had an agreement—or are humans really dishonest infidels? Answer me, Captain! Your life is forfeit if you have no explanation."

Kirk's eyes snapped, but he controlled his anger. If the situation were reversed he would react as S'Talon had—possibly with less restraint.

"Commander. Is it true none of the shots have landed?"

"That is true," conceded the Romulan.

"Shot down by our own vessels?"

S'Talon inclined his head.

"And are those same vessels deployed in front of your ships, shielding them?"

"Yes."

"Then please listen to me, Commander. The Federation is the victim of a mutiny. The *Potemkin* is under attack from within. Her captain has ordered the ship's destruction if the mutineer refuses to surrender. If just one shot hits there'll be war. Neither of us wants that. Nor do I want to see the *Potemkin* destroyed."

"What can be done?"

"Speak to your superiors. Convince them to give us time. We have reason to believe this communication is being monitored—by the man responsible for the attack. He refuses to believe the Federation and the Romulan empire can work together. If we can show him the truth we might be able to reason with him. Will you help, Commander?"

"Of course. It is in my best interest, and that of the empire. Without the Canarans' gran my people will die. We need your cooperation, Captain, and that of the Federation. We will not attack unless one of our ships is hit and we will guarantee your safety unless war is declared. I pledge it."

"Thank you, Commander. I can ask no more."

"Luck, Captain."

"For all of us, Commander," replied Kirk as the Romulan departed. "Well, Mister Spock?"

"That should be efficacious, Captain. If the communication was heard."

"And if it's been relayed to Iota." Kirk rubbed his hands together. "Now we wait," he said.

S'Talon walked down the corridor, seething at the Praetor's ability to anger him. The man was an overblown, pompous egotist who should be told his own miniscule value in the scheme of things. If only he were not so dangerous . . . amazing how position and power enforced respect, even when it was not deserved. He had had to beg this time and the overstuffed windbag had enjoyed it! He had smiled his fat smile and wallowed in his power. His thoughts increased the force of S'Talon's footsteps. The humiliation he endured had better be worth it, he thought savagely. "Peace at any price" he had as much as stated to the Terran captain, but some prices were too high—self-respect, dignity. The void take Kirk anyhow!

A wave of frustration rolled over the Romulan at the thought of his Terran counterpart. Kirk had persuaded him into all of this. He knew he could not have managed it on his own. Well, he had a choice. He could refuse to cooperate, but that would solve nothing. He had agreed to Kirk's plan because it was the only possible course of action. And Kirk was at least a man of some principle. It was ironic that he found himself better able to work with his enemies than his own people. S'Talon growled to himself. Once more he had spliced the fragile threads of understanding. He was not adept at diplomacy, yet he was always embroiled in its sticky web. He shrugged, mentally casting off subterfuge and deceit. He craved action. Once the plague was contained he would request a transfer to the dangerous exploratory missions on the edges of Romulan space. He had no doubt the Praetor would grant his request.

Mikel Garson stood on the bridge of the *Potemkin*. His face was white and drawn, the muscles of his jaw contracted. Strain showed in his eyes and in the tense, compressed line of his mouth. He twisted his hands together behind his back. He had no doubt he would have to destroy the ship. The *Potemkin* had become a floating prison, four hundred and thirty people trapped within its hull. A part of Iota's assault was a power cut in "unnecessary systems"—systems like the transporter—so he could channel more energy into the weapons banks. Garson did not want to die and he loathed the thought of murdering his crew. They had signed on aware of the possibility of death, but he would order their destruction. It was murder and he could not stomach it.

"Get me the admiral," he said tersely. "And I want it visual this time."

He would try again to talk some sense into that bonehead . . . until the last moment he would try.

"Admiral Iota!"

"Don't bother me, Garson."

Iota's smug voice drove the captain to distraction.

"Iota, you are a fool! You're throwing away a chance that could be the beginning of peace!"

"Garson, you make me tired. And you're insubordinate. I will not forget when this is over."

"You won't have a chance to remember! This ship will be destroyed in . . . twelve point four-two minutes."

"Bah! You're bluffing. You don't have the courage for that. Now leave me alone before I . . ."

The admiral's voice trailed off as a high-pitched, intermittent beep sounded. He pressed a lever on his wrist communicator.

"What is it?" Iota asked.

"Admiral, I think you should hear this . . . I think we were wrong," said a distant voice.

"Proceed with the communication."

Iota bent to catch the taped communiqué and Captain Garson's heart leaped. Kirk! He prayed for a miracle. Time was suspended, interminable. The admiral's silver hair was alive with white highlights, the rugged line of his cheek impassive, broad shoulders drooping a little with fatigue. His head sank lower and lower. To the captain's hopeful eyes there was defeat in the humility of his posture. Iota raised his head and turned away.

"The victory is yours, Captain," he said in a muffled voice. "It seems I was wrong."

Garson controlled the tremor in his voice.

"Admiral, you will allow security to escort you to your quarters."

Iota did not speak, but nodded his acquiescence. Garson turned from the viewscreen, his grey eyes alive with victory.

"Ensign Heery, abort destruct order."

"Yes, sir!"

The smile in Heery's voice was symptomatic of the relief flooding the bridge.

"Commander Yellowhorse, get me Tiercellus."

Yellowhorse looked up from the communications board.

"Sir, the Romulans say the detachment is now led by a Commander Hexce. He's on, sir."

"This is the *Potemkin*. Our emergency situation is under control. Repeat, we have complete control."

"I am glad to hear that, Captain. Only the Praetor's orders saved you," answered Hexce.

"Your discipline has been noted, sir," replied Garson.

"It was wearing thin."

"It will be tried no further. Though I acknowledge my debt to you, I cannot refrain from pointing out the Federation's patience has been your ally."

"And I acknowledge the truth of what you say—reluctantly. We will keep the truce," answered Hexce.

"As will we," said Garson.

Hexce favored the Terran with the Romulan salute, indicating the end of the discussion as far as he was concerned. The screen replaced his image with its former survey of the four enemy ships.

Captain Garson sank into his command chair.

"Maintain position," he said.

"Aye, sir."

Garson closed his eyes. No more, he thought. If this isn't the end I don't want to be told. He let his mind slip quietly away to linger over the ideal shore leave.

"Journal: the fifth day of Esaan."

Romm Joramm's stylus traced the sweeping curves of Canaran script with practiced ease.

"Canara has sustained a time of crisis. That is over. The danger was great . . . we ran the risk of extinction . . . but if we learned from what we have gone through, I venture to say the benefits may outweigh the dangers. For the first time Canara has dealt with

216

true outsiders—enemies—and survived. We had help and examples, both good and bad.

"For myself, I find it hard to view the Romulan envoy S'Talon as an enemy. Unlike his Praetor, he is concerned for the welfare of others, and I have always found it difficult to accept a role instead of an individual. Perhaps this betrays a certain lack of experience and worldliness on my part. No matter. I am an old man. When younger, more flexible minds carry the weight of leadership they will find answers to questions I never dreamed of asking.

"The harvest is almost complete, and the production of a vaccine is underway in the laboratory Doctor McCoy has set up. This is a most interesting development. With our supply of gran it would be beneficial to have more and larger laboratories to manufacture medicine here on Canara. Doctor McCoy and I have spoken of this in depth and he feels that gran itself should be studied more carefully. He has obtained a supply for personal research, but he feels it deserves the full attention of a competent laboratory for no less than five years! Imagine—we know only one-tenth of gran's potential!"

The script wavered as the old man's hand shook with enthusiasm.

"A vast new world opens before us. It is diverse and challenging, full of opportunity, but to take advantage of it we will have to curb our headstrong impulses. I very nearly destroyed Canara through my own selfish sense of injury. That most arresting young Captain Kirk has given me a glimpse of Canara's future. Through his eyes I have seen the limitless possibilities open to our young people. We have much to learn, but I am confident we will win through. There is much to be done."

Joramm initialed the entry and closed the journal. He leaned back, tilting his head up to the sky, though he knew neither the *Enterprise* nor the Romulan fleet was visible to the naked eye. These young men had excited him—so intense, so dedicated to their goals. He had been like that once. He chuckled suddenly, realizing he still was. Well, peace follow them all. He, meanwhile, had a harvest to see to.

"Captain's log: stardate three-one three-zero point four.

"The Romulan crisis is under control. Commander S'Talon has come to an understanding with the Canarans and the Romulan empire has agreed to buy their entire supply of gran. Doctor McCoy estimates that, made into the new vaccine, it will be enough to stem the myrruthesian plague . . ."

"Captain," interrupted Uhura, "Commander S'Talon wishes to speak to you."

"Thank you, Lieutenant," answered Kirk. "Main viewscreen."

S'Talon's image materialized, his profile cutting a clean line against the shadowy red of his quarters. He was alone, and for a moment he seemed lost in thought, but when he turned his eyes locked with Kirk's.

"Doctor McCoy, Mister Spock . . . Captain," he acknowledged.

"Commander," returned Kirk.

"Our work here is almost complete. Soon we will return home and the cooperation we have enjoyed will dissolve. We will be enemies with the Neutral Zone a wall between us and there will be little opportunity for personal feeling. James Kirk, not only are you and your crew directly responsible for stopping a war and keeping a civilization from decimation by disease, you have secured my position as well."

Kirk opened his mouth to reply, but S'Talon continued.

"I believe, Captain, you would make as valuable a friend as you are dangerous an enemy. Whatever circumstances may require of me, I remain in your debt . . . I will remember, Captain."

"Good-bye, S'Talon, my friend," said Kirk. The Romulan Commander's eyes were full of regret as he faded from the screen.

"That's quite a man, Jim," said McCoy with respect. "His medical knowledge is phenomenal."

"It is regrettable we are on opposite sides," acknowledged Spock. "Commander S'Talon is a remarkable personality. When I questioned him about his ship, he merely replied he had personally set a delayed action overload in sequence before he left her and that the Federation would find nothing but microscopic debris."

"His concern is for the welfare of his people," mused Kirk, "just as our concern is for the welfare of ours. Yet we are enemies. No logic in it, is there, Spock?"

"War, in all its forms, is not a logical process," said Spock, his eyes dark.

"No," answered the captain. He punched into the computer to finish the log entry S'Talon had interrupted. "Our mission is successfully completed and the *Enterprise* will be leaving the area in approximately four point two-three hours, when we will proceed to the nearest Starbase for computer repair. Kirk out."

"Recorded, my darling, my dearest," answered the computer in its most seductive tones. "Another brilliant mission completed by my brave, loyal, warm . . ."

The computer continued its list of adjectives as the captain's face fell.

"Spock . . ." he said in a desperate, tiny voice.

Spock's lips twitched.

"I am sorry, Captain," said Spock with conciliatory sympathy, "but the log entries are directly tied to the library computer and I can do nothing until it is reprogrammed . . ."

Kirk lowered his head, his forehead resting on the heel of one hand. He was the picture of helpless dejection.

". . . noble, loving, hardworking . . ." the computer continued.

Kirk's whole body sank.

"Look at it this way, Jim: she may be a machine, but she's all yours," McCoy chuckled.

"You did say you loved her, Captain."

Spock's voice was innocent.

Uhura turned quickly to her communications board, choked by an irrepressible giggle. Sulu shook with silent laughter and Chekov had to clamp his mouth shut. The bridge was violently quiet when a chortle erupted from the command chair. The chortle bubbled into a laugh and the bridge exploded . . . except, of course, for Spock. He observed the situation with innocence and mild surprise . . . his own approach to humor.

". . . pure, kind and generous, my own true love," the computer finished fondly, totally unaware of the reaction it was causing.

The *Enterprise* rocked with laughter.

THE CRY OF THE ONLIES

Boaco Six — a once tranquil Federation colony, is caught in the throes of revolution. The Enterprise's™ mission: re-establish contact and determine whether diplomatic ties should be strengthened.

Negotiations are proceeding smoothly, until the goodwill is shattered by the destruction of a Boacan ship — at the hands of an experimental Starfleet vessel!

Now, to prevent war, The Enterprise™ must recapture the stolen vessel, a mission requiring the aid of a reclusive genius — and bringing Kirk face-to-face with the long buried secrets of his past…

DWELLERS IN THE CRUCIBLE

Warrantors of Peace: the Federation's daring
experiment to prevent war among its members.
Each Warrantor, man or woman, is hostage for
the government of his native world — and is
instantly killed if that world breaks the peace.

Now Romulans have kidnapped six
Warrantors, to foment political chaos — and
then civil war — within the Federation. Captain
Kirk must send Sulu to infiltrate Romulan
territory, find the hostages and bring them back
alive — before the Federation self destructs!

Available now from Titan Books

THE CAPTAINS' HONOUR

A series of vicious attacks by the alien Kzinti
has devastated the planet Tenara — bringing
the Enterprise™ and another Federation
starship, the Centurion, to the planet's aid. The
Centurion's captain is Lucius Sejanus — a
powerful, magnetic man whose crew seems
more dedicated to him than to the ideals of the
Federation. Sejanus wants to carry the battle
back to the Kzinti home planet — and several of
the Enterprise's™ officers want to join him.

But unknown to anyone, Sejanus plans to
escalate the conflict into full scale war. A war
from which he will emerge a hero — primed to
seize control of the Federation itself...

If you have difficulty obtaining any of the Star Trek range of books, you can order direct from Titan Books Mail Order, 58 St Giles High St, London WC2H 8LH. Tel: (01) 497 2150.

Star Trek novels	£2.95 each
Star Trek: The Next Generation novels	£2.95 each
Star Trek Giant novels	£3.95 each
The *Star Trek* Compendium	£7.95
Mr Scott's Guide to the Enterprise	£6.95
The *Star Trek* Interview Book	£5.95

For postage & packing: on orders up to £5 add £1.20; orders up to £10 add £2.00; orders up to £15 add £2.50; orders up to £20 add £2.70; orders over £20 add £3.00. Make cheques or postal orders payable to Titan Books. NB. UK customers only.

While every effort is made to keep prices steady, Titan Books reserves the right to change cover prices at short notice from those listed here.